MY GOD!
MY COUNTRY,
MY SON

My God! My Country, My Son
Copyright © 2018 Peter Ford

Ford Publishing

Book design by:
Arbor Services, Inc.
www.arborservices.co/

Printed in the United States of America

My God! My Country, My Son
Peter Ford

1. Title 2. Author 3. Historical Fiction

Library of Congress Control Number: 2017912958
ISBN 13: 978-0-692-93842-3

MY GOD!
MY COUNTRY,
MY SON

PETER FORD

Ford Publishing

This book is dedicated to my father,
Peter A. Ford II, the Soldiers who have fought for the freedoms
that we now enjoy and those who continue to stand for freedom,
justice and equality.

Contents

Acknowledgement

I am extremely grateful to all the wonderful people who have inspired and encouraged me throughout the writing of this book. As much I would like to acknowledge you all, I can only mention a few. I would like to begin with my father Peter Ford Sr., the artist who created me; my mother, Johnnie Blackman who brought me into this world and cared for me. I thank my brother and sister Stephan Platt, Schila Washington and Cynthia Ford who gave me support in all my endeavors.

They say it takes a village to raise a child, so I would like to thank all the women of McGehee, Arkansas, who didn't spare the rod to spoil this child. I would like to acknowledge my aunt Melvina Newhouse for showing me strength and faith. I would like to thank my aunt Billie Neal, who took me in and comforted me through some of my darkest days.

Life is sometimes like a roller coaster ride, it has its ups and its downs. It is where those lows in life where true friendship and love can be found. I thank my wife Delonda for finding me, like the winds of a hurricane she came and swept me off my feet, she is the drum major that added rhythm to my lonely heartbeat.

Thank you Church Without Walls for walking with me on the road to salvation and teaching me the purpose of life—God, apart from him I can do nothing.

I would also like to thank the Veteran's Administration in Richmond, Texas for diagnosing my struggle with depression and treating it.

I would like to thank the people at Arbor Publishing for making this possible: Olga, Larry, Lori, and Rick; for doing a phenomenal job.

I would like to acknowledge my baby girl Alexis, my son Kevin and daughter Xandria Ford for opening my eyes to another part of me.

Thank you, Morgan, Madison and Myles Johnson, for helping me find my smile again.

Thanks to my nephews and nieces: Stephan, Eric, Dominic, and Danielle Platt, Kristen Washington, and Jonathan Blackman for always believing in me.

Prologue

Children of an all-black school recite the pledge of allegiance, with their hands over their hearts as dark clouds and strong winds loom over the indigent community of colored people.

"Good morning class," said Dr. Davis a light-skinned black man, who is one of the most revered persons in the community. "Today we are going to talk about the Jim Crow Laws and one of the most important speeches in American history," he continued.

"Does anyone know the history of Jim Crow or how the Jim Crow Laws were established," asked Dr. Davis.

The students in the class were silent. They knew of the Jim Crow Laws; but did not know how they were established.

Dr. Davis holds his hands in front of his face as if praying… "Let me rearticulate that question.

Can anyone tell me about the Jim Crow Laws," asked Davis.

Will Wanton raises hand and speaks, "It is the law that provides facilities for black folks to use just like the ones white folks use."

Yes, Mr. Wanton that is correct; but I must ask (as he scans the room), are the facilities equal, Mister Odom," Asked Davis?

"Of course, they are equal," Pee Wee Odom answered. "Both bathrooms have toilets, don't they?"

"If Mr. Odom is correct, can anyone explain, why white folks have school buildings and we are taught in churches and barns," asked Davis? "Therefore, the reality of the Jim Crow Laws are separate and unequal," Davis continued.

Dr. Davis removed his glasses and put them on his desk. "People, you are the future and there are some things that you must understand and stand for," implored Davis.

"Understand that nothing in this world is free, not even freedom," explains Davis. "Therefore, I implore you to stand and fight for your God given rights, which served as the basis on which the U.S. Constitution was written."

Davis continued, "Abraham Lincoln recited one of the most important speeches in U.S history during the American Civil War in 1863. It is called the Gettysburg Address." Listen to these words. "Four score and seven years ago, our fathers brought forth on this continent a new nation: conceived in Liberty, and dedicated to the proposition that all men are created equal."

"Many of our forefathers have died for our freedoms and now it is up to us to fight for equality," implored Davis.

"Do you remember the poem Freedom's Plow by Langston Hughes," asked Davis?

Young Pee Wee Odom jokingly replied, "A long time ago but not so long ago, a lot of men said and did a lot of things."

"Thank you for that comedic interpretation, Mr. Odom, but I am looking for a more substantive answer," replied Davis.

Little Will Wanton raised his hand and stood once Dr. Davis pointed to him and began to speak. It seems to me that freedom was a birthright to some in this country, while others had to work for it, some fought for it, and some even died for it. I think the poem Freedom's Plow is about how people from all races worked and sacrificed to make this a great nation.

"Yes! Young Mr. Wanton, yes," replied Davis, "that is exactly what the poem was about, it was a rallying cry for an oppressed people and the ways they came to this country and worked for their freedom."

"I find this poem interesting because it is rooted in the word," explains Davis. "Romans 8:20-22, says that we have been groaning since childbirth up to the present time. We cannot stand idly by and wait; we must work for what we want in our hearts. The bible also reminds us in James 2:14-26; faith without work is dead."

A kid runs into the school yelling, "Dr. Davis! Dr. Davis!" Davis grabs the kid by the arm, "hold on young man, what's all the commotion?"

The kid pulls a note from a torn pocket of his dirty jeans and gives it to Dr. Davis. The doctor unfolds the note, reads it, and puts it on his desk.

"Okay class, I have been informed that a severe storm is heading this way, therefore, I must release you to go home....so, class dismissed," Davis explained.

The kids cheered, put their books away and began to exit the building. Young Will walks up to Davis, taps him on the shoulder; Davis turned and looked at him.

"Dr. Davis are you still going to give me music lessons tonight," asked Will.

Dr. Davis smiles, looks at Young Will and replies, "Yes young Will, you are my most promising student. Come on over tonight if it is okay with your parents."

Will started walking toward the exit; Davis calls him back. Will slowly turns and walk over to Davis. The doctor puts his hand on Will's shoulder.

"Will, one day our generation is going to fade away and each generation needs someone to stand for what's right and speak for those who cannot be heard. Therefore, I give you this, it is called The Word, if you hold on to these teachings, you will know the truth and the truth will set you free.

Puzzled by Davis' words, Will looks at him and walks toward the door.

Davis calls out, Will you have that fire burning inside of you and one day you will be a torch to lead your generation to live in a nation of a more perfect union.

Once out of the building, Will runs to catch up with Pee Wee. Will almost out of breath, "Look at what Dr. Davis gave me, holding his book up in the air. He said the teachings in this book will lead our generation into a more perfect union."

Pee Wee laughs, "Dr. Davis is really doing a job on your head, the only teaching you need from Dr. Davis is those guitar lessons so we can make our music."

Later that evening, Dr. Davis walks into his home out of the streaming rain only to find his wife on her knees praying. "Honey, what's going on, asked Davis. Startled, Mrs. Davis jumps up runs to her husband and embraces him in her arms.

"The police! The police and some Soldiers came here looking for you," she replied.

"What?" asked Dr. Davis. "We have to move, start packing!" Davis commanded as he runs to the closet and starts throwing clothes into a trunk at the rear of his bed.

Mrs. Davis stands in front of her husband impeding him from pulling more clothes from the closet trying to find out why the police and soldiers were looking for him.

Dr. Davis grabs his wife by both her arms looks her directly in her eyes and says, "Honey, I was on the front line protesting black men being sent off to war to fight for a country that does not recognize them as equals and my number came up in the draft. I refuse to fight for a country that denies me fair and equal treatment, so I ran away."

"What? Are you a fugitive?" Asked Mrs. Davis.

"No honey, I am a conscientious objector, I will explain it all to you later after we get out of here," explained Davis as he continued throwing clothes into his trunk.

They hear a knock at the door, Dr. Davis ducks into the closet and signals his wife to go and answer the door. Mrs. Davis opens the door and yells to her husband, "Honey, it is Will."

Dr. Davis breathes a sigh of relief, and tells his wife to let little Will in. Will walks into the house with rain dripping from his clothes.

"Are you leaving," asked Will.

Davis puts hands on Will's shoulders and looks him in the eyes, "yes, Will we are but I have something to give you before we go."

Davis reaches into the closet, pulls out his guitar case puts it on the table and opens it. "This is yours to remember me by, but I want you to promise me something," said Davis.

"Anything Dr. Davis, anything," said Will.

"Practice. Remember the Freedom's Plow. Study the word and hold on to its teachings," exclaimed Davis.

A loud and thunderous noise is heard at the door as the police traverse. Dr. Davis pushes Will to the side and tries to escape through the back door only to get captured by the police waiting for him on the other side of the door.

Mrs. Davis and Will try to help to no avail because some of the police are restraining them as the other police officers escort Dr. Davis away.

"Guard in your heart the seed planted by Thomas Jefferson and stand little Will stand!" screamed Davis. "I love you honey, they can take me but they can't take the love that I have for you," Davis continued.

Chapter One

The dream always started with him staring into the darkness, surrounded by smoke and the smell of death. He knew it instinctually. Will Wanton's animal sense made his dreams seem so real, as if he could feel the flames of fire hidden by the plumes of smoke in the air.

In the distance, Will could see silhouettes of fighting soldiers outlined by the tense flames of a powerful fire. Friendly soldiers retreated toward the town as the enemy advanced.

One friendly soldier was hit by shrapnel in the back as another, shot in the leg, fell to the ground. Still another friendly soldier entered an abandoned warehouse on the edge of town.

Somehow, Will felt himself moving away from the action. He felt a connection, a need to know what was about to happen. He looked over the war-torn village—to see only one house standing with a single light glowing in the window. Everything else was shrouded in darkness.

Will stepped toward the action and found himself on the stage of a colored-only club. Some people in the club danced to the music of the band. Others sat at tables playing cards, dominoes, and drinking in the lively atmosphere.

With a final riff, Will slung his guitar over his back and jumped offstage. Hands reached out as people patted him on the back. He made his way through the crowd, grinning as people complimented him and the band on their last set of the night.

In the corner of the room, beneath the exit sign, stood a beautiful, light-skinned girl with brown hair and wide brown eyes. Her generous lips curved into a smile as their eyes met.

Will slowly moved toward her but was stopped by a young man organizing an equal rights rally the next day. The young man asked Will if he and the band could perform at the rally. Torn by passion, Will halfheartedly listened to the man while trying to keep track of the girl. In an act of desperation to get away, he agreed to sing at the rally. However, when he looked back toward the exit sign, the girl was gone.

Will made his way to the exit and opened the door to see if the girl was in the alley way. Stepping into the cold, deserted alley, which was usually filled with club patrons, the door swung shut behind him. The alley was dim, except for the green light flickering above the dangling sign: Club 6661. Now in the middle of the desolate alley, Will was frightened but tried to maintain his cool, thinking his friends were playing a practical joke.

Walking back to the door, Will knocked a couple of times. "Come on, man, whoever is holding the door, let it go. All right? This is very funny! Let me in."

Something moved behind him. He turned and saw a dark silhouette running toward the opposite end of the alley. Unable to resist, he ran after it. The distance between Will, the man, and the club seemed to get longer and longer. Following the silhouette, Will ran out into an empty, rain-slicked street. A stoplight flickered red, casting light on the figure that stood in the center of the intersection.

The soldier stood holding his rifle, looking and listening for the enemy as blood streamed down his face. As Will approached, he recognized the man's face.

"Dad?" Will cried in horror. "Dad!"

In desperation, Will attempted to save his father as a tank powered through the intersection, cannons pointed toward his dad. The tank fired a loud shot as Will reached for his father. As Will was about to touch his father, he screamed, "No!" and was blown back by the impact of the blast.

Will was jolted awake by his father as his mother stumbled into the doorway. "Boy, what the hell is wrong with you?" his father asked. "In here screaming like a . . . I don't know where you got that from, but you didn't get it from me."

"I think that's enough," said Gloria Wanton as she interrupted her husband. She narrowed her eyes as she looked at him. She sat down on the edge of the bed next to Will and gave him a hug. "It's okay, sweetheart. We heard you hollering from the other room. You had another nightmare, dear?"

Will nodded.

"That's a damn shame," said the embarrassed father. "Grown-assed man waking up in the middle of the night screaming!"

He left, slamming the door behind him.

"Ignore him, son. He doesn't think men should have emotions. He was raised to believe that, you know. He is stubborn as a mule when it comes to his beliefs," explained Will's mom.

"Yeah, I know, he is a special kind of man," Will replied.

"And you are something else too," replied Mrs. Wanton. "You are just as stubborn as your father."

His mother kissed his forehead and left the room. Will sat up in his bed for a while lightly strumming his guitar. The longer he stayed awake, the faster the details of the dream receded. Disturbed by the dream, Will managed to make it through the rest of the night without having another nightmare.

Early the next morning Will met his best friend Pee Wee Odom at the bus stop. They would normally ride the bus to their old elementary school for rehearsal. However, this morning, they were riding the bus to meet the band at the park to participate in an equal rights rally. It was springtime, and the mild weather lent itself to outdoor gatherings. Will knew his father, a true patriot, wouldn't approve of his being at a rally of this kind. The rally had been organized to protest the separate but equal Jim Crow laws.

A few blocks from his home, signs of the Jim Crow laws were apparent and too obvious. The separate but equal signs had been put into place to remind colored people that they were second-class citizens, not good enough to use the same facilities as whites. The farther the bus moved from the colored side of town, the more Will saw the detested inequality of society. But as tired as he was of unfair rules, he was just as tired of seeing colored people so ready to comply with them. It was like they lived their lives wearing blinders, unaware of what was going on. Will often wondered how his people could accept being treated as second-class citizens and what it would take to make these people wake up. Stories about unjust crimes ruled the news in black neighborhoods—cops beating colored men for next to nothing, or black men found hung somewhere in the wilderness by what appeared to be a Klan killing. Other than these violent and horrific occurrences, most colored people kept their eyes down and smiled when addressed by whites. They moved through life obeying an unfair set of rules, afraid that shaking up the status quo would only draw negative consequences.

The separate but equal laws were stamped on every business downtown, prompting Will to think about the poem "Freedom's Plow" by Langston Hughes. Pee Wee fumbled with his trumpet and rambled about being famous the whole ride, as usual. The bus turned the corner onto the army base. Pee Wee looked out the window, rubbed his chin, sighed deeply, and mumbled, "Hold on, keep your hands on the plow."

Will had lived most of his life in Camp Campbell, and the sights were depressingly familiar to him. It was 1950, and as far back as Will could remember, life in Camp Campbell had not changed much. The bus route went from one side of town to the other, originating in the side of town where colored folk lived. The end of the line was downtown in the business district. Many of the colored people who lived in the city worked downtown, but the restaurants refused to serve them. The No Coloreds Allowed signs were everywhere. He was used to seeing them, but these days their presence raised Will's awareness of equality and the Gettysburg Address by Abraham Lincoln, which reiterated the principles of equality espoused by the Declaration of Independence.

Sitting on the back of the bus was an everyday occurrence for colored people, and if it got crowded and a white person entered the bus, a colored person had to give up his seat or risk being shipped off to jail. There were so many rules. You didn't look white people in the eye or speak to them unless spoken to, and you don't dare look at white women. Black men were to keep their eyes on the ground when passing a white woman. Will heard enough stories and saw pictures in the newspaper to know what happened to colored men who didn't comply with the rules. It was exceedingly easy to get killed if you were a colored man.

In some ways, Will didn't feel at home unless he was in the neighborhood with his own people, where he was treated equally. At least there, he didn't have to fear his every action.

Will sighed and scooted down in his seat as the city bus rolled onto the army base. He saw several formations of colored soldiers marching.

"Ah man," Will said. He always cringed when the bus came up Birch Street. It was too close to his father's company for his liking.

"What's wrong?" Pee Wee asked.

"You'll see in a minute," he said. "Watch the soldier who is sitting three seats in front of us."

The young colored soldier a few seats ahead of them stood and swallowed over the lump in his throat as the bus neared the next stop. He ran to the exit when the bus stopped and jumped out the door as soon as the driver opened it. He ran across the street and tried to join the formation without anyone noticing him.

"And here we go in three, two, one . . . ," Will whispered.

Sergeant First Class Wanton saw the soldier and shouted in a loud, thunderous voice.

"Who in the hell do you think you are?" he yelled, pointing his finger in the soldier's face. "Soldier, if I catch you late to my formation again, I will stick my boot so far up your ass you'll be coughing up Kiwi for the rest of your life. Do you understand me?"

"Yes, Sergeant!" the soldier replied.

"Your dad is the man," Pee Wee said excitedly. "Getting those troops in line."

Will's lip curled upward in disgust. "You don't get it, do you?"

The bus pulled away from that stop and slowly moved down the street. Will pulled the cord for the next stop. Neither man spoke again until they were on the sidewalk, away from the people on the bus. People knew Will's dad around town, and he was careful about airing his opinion of him, in case word got back around. The last thing he needed was his father hearing some comment he made and getting mad about it. He was perpetually upset about one thing or another.

"What don't I get?" Pee Wee asked.

"My father, he's just another Tom being used as a pawn, helping the man keep black people in line, and the worst thing about it—he doesn't even know it," Will explained.The park was only a couple of blocks from the bus stop. They walked over to the rest of the waiting band members. Though he'd been concerned about running late, Will's worries were soon calmed by the warm reception he and Pee Wee received. They were well-known among the colored community.

Pushing their way through the crowd, Will and Pee Wee made it to the stage. Will couldn't help but pick up on the happy vibe. Adults danced and laughed while children played on the see saws and slides. A clown made balloon animals and handed them out to the kids. Looking out from the vantage point of the bandstand he saw the homemade signs the people waved: All Men Are Created Equal, Justice for All, and A House Divided Against Itself Cannot Stand.

"Lift Every Voice and Sing," Will said to the band, then signaled to the drummer, who started up a beat. He clapped his hands and encouraged the crowd to join in. When Pee Wee lifted his horn, the bassist and guitar player played along.

Whenever he sang with the band, Will felt transported to another place. Stage fright melted the moment he got into the rhythm of a song. It made him feel alive, gave him purpose. Performing at equal rights rallies was even more rewarding than the gigs they performed at local clubs. Here, it was about connecting in a different way. It was about uplifting the crowd and having hope for the future. Since the cause was more important, he put his soul into the songs they sang that day. While on stage, Will reflected on the things Dr. Davis had tried to teach them before the military took him away. Dr. Davis had given Will a crystal clear purpose in life— to use the tools of music; knowledge of the colonized mind; and ways to free the mind, body, and soul.

Every moment on stage seemed long, yet when it ended it seemed gone too soon. Will grinned at Pee Wee as the audience clapped loudly. Descending the stage, Will mopped the sweat from his face and noticed a cluster of white soldiers in uniform. He smiled, knowing that he had taken the first step to freeing himself by publicly singing about inequality and trying to wake people from being enslaved by a colonized mind.

"Man, we knocked them dead!" Pee Wee said. "Did you see how they were moving? We had the crowd going wild with that song."

Will nodded. "Well, that's what music's all about: soothing the soul, bringing out the emotions and spirits of people, filling them with passion, joy, and hope, which is exactly what this country needs."

Pee Wee twirled his trumpet. "I've been telling you for the longest time we need to go ahead and cut that album, man. We could be rich."

"That's not what music is about," Will said. "It should be about freedom, creativity, and self-expression; doing God's will."

"All that's well and good, but not worth a damn if you're not getting paid," Pee Wee said.

"What good does it profit a man to gain the world but lose his soul?" Will asked. "I can't sell my soul for a dollar."

Pee Wee fell into step beside Will as they walked through the crowd. This was a recurring topic of conversation between the two of them: Pee Wee thought they should do something more with their music, while Will was convinced that a record deal would mean enslavement to a record company, loss of creative control, and selling out like his father. Heavily influenced by Dr. Davis, Will felt a man should stand by his beliefs, regardless of the cost. The last thing he wanted was anyone telling him what kind of music he should play or what types of songs he should sing.

"Hey, hold up," Pee Wee said, stopping him. "I'm suddenly feeling a bit hungry, and I know just what I want."

Will followed Pee Wee's gaze to a girl standing a few feet away. She was in line at the hamburger stand, her back turned away from them. Pee Wee ran a hand over his processed hair.

"You have a pencil and paper?" Pee Wee asked.

"Yes. Why?" Will replied.

"You might want to take notes." Pee Wee grinned. "I am about to show you how to catch fresh fish." He politely pushed Will to the side and approached the girl.

Will smirked, took a deep breath, and followed him to the burger stand. He wondered if Pee Wee was trying to be discreet, because it was obvious he was staring at the girl's rear. The girl was big boned and shapely. She appeared not to notice either of them and was engrossed in reading the menu.

"Strawberry lemonade, medium, please," she said with a smile, handing the menu back to the man behind the counter. "And for my hamburger . . ."

"Do you come here often?" Pee Wee interrupted.

The girl turned, gave Pee Wee a cynical glare, and replied, "Only when I have a taste for a good hamburger." She turned her attention back to the cashier and completed her order.

Pee Wee twirled his trumpet, holding it close to his lips. "What do you suggest?" he asked, undeterred by the fact the girl was ignoring him.

In a quick glance, she took him in from head to toe. She gave him a sarcastic grin. "For you, I recommend the kid's meal."

Will shook his head, trying to hold his laughter in. He felt bad for his friend---it was so clear he wasn't getting anywhere with this girl.

A determined Pee Wee took a couple of steps back with his eyes glued on the girl's derriere.

The girl paid for her meal, took it from the cashier, and sat at a nearby table. Pee Wee followed her. As she reached inside the bag to retrieve her food, Pee Wee uttered, "Mm, mm, mm, that looks delicious."

The girl turned around and held up her hamburger. "Are you talking about this?" she asked.

"No. I'm talking about that." Pee Wee motioned to the girl's rear.

With a flick of her head, she turned, looking over her shoulder at her own behind. Then she looked at Pee Wee and shook her head. "Ah, no. You can't handle that; it's way too much for you." She paused for a moment. "You know, you have big dreams for such a little man."

"What's wrong with dreams?" Pee Wee asked. "Dreams are merely aspirations of the self-conscious mind; what harm is there to dream about you and believe in the possibilities of us?"

Will, with a smirk on his face, moved past Pee Wee and leaned on a banister near the girl's table.

"I have a big appetite, and you got just what I want," Pee Wee said. "Girl, the things I could do with you."

"By the looks of things," she said, "you can't do too much."

Will couldn't help it. The large gulp of soda he'd just taken exploded from his mouth as he laughed. Pee Wee didn't flinch or even pause. He seemed convinced he was going to get the girl to talk to him. Her words seemed not to affect him at all.

"I may have a small frame, but baby, I am all beef," Pee Wee replied.

"Those are pretty big words coming from such a small package," she countered.

"This package is big enough to turn you out," Pee Wee replied.

"You can talk up a good game, but can you play one?" she asked.

"There's only one way to find out," Pee Wee said.

"I hear you talking. What do they call you anyway?" she asked.

Pee Wee twirled his trumpet, tapped his lips to the mouthpiece, and tried to say his name in a sexy tone. "Pee Wee."

The girl cracked up as soda spewed from her mouth. She stood up, put one hand on his shoulder, and bent at the waist, laughing until tears popped from her eyes.

"Where on earth did you get a name like that?"

"From my dad," he said.

"You should ask him to take it back," she replied, still laughing.

Will walked away, shaking his head. It was too painful to watch his friend strike out.

"I'm sorry," she said. "My name is Bertha." After she calmed down, she looked into his eyes with a smirk on her face. She seemed surprised to realize how close he was standing to her. If Pee Wee had been taller, it could have been said they were shoulder to shoulder.

"So," he said just above a whisper, "are you going to let me grind that beef or what?"

Bertha's mouth dropped open in surprise, because for once in her life she didn't have the last word. Pee Wee smiled.

Later that afternoon, SFC William Wanton Sr. entered the kitchen to have lunch with his wife, Gloria. She usually had a good meal prepared for him. Lunch with his wife was important to him, because it gave him time to wind down from the stress of the morning and gave him energy to make it through the rest of the day. Wanton kissed Gloria on the cheek and sat at the table.

Gloria got up, put fried chicken, mashed potatoes, and collard greens on a plate, and placed it on the table in front of him. She sat back at the table and continued to slice peaches into a big white bowl. Usually she ate lunch with him, but she was too busy slicing peaches for the cobbler she was making for dessert. They sat in silence for a while. Sunshine drifted in through the kitchen window, beaming on her head as if heaven was touching her mind. There were brown highlights in her dark hair, as well as a few shimmery threads of silver on her crown. To William, Gloria was beautiful, even more so than the day they married. He'd been nineteen, and she was only seventeen on the day they declared their love for one another to the world. Children really, though they had all the responsibilities of grown folk. He never failed to see the shadow of the girl remaining within her, even as he adored the mature woman she had become. Time had changed them both, and he loved her even more because they had stood the test of time together.

Gloria noticed William picking at his food. She set down the knife and asked, "What's wrong, dear?" "I was thinking about Will. I just don't understand him," Wanton replied.

"What do you mean?" Gloria asked, putting aside the bowl. "He's no different than any other boy his age."

"I don't know," Wanton said. "He just doesn't act like the rest of the young men around here. The only thing he cares about is playing that damn guitar." Gloria put her hands on the table. "What's wrong with that? You spend most of your time with your soldiers."

"That's true, but my time is used to provide for this family," said Wanton. "Will, on the other hand, does nothing but walk around with that guitar slung over his back wearing those funny-looking clothes. The boy is twenty years old, doesn't have a job, and is still living with us."

Gloria stood up and put her hands on her hips. "What is he supposed to do?"

"Get a job, do something constructive. Anything is better than being a starving artist."

"How do you know he doesn't get paid?" Gloria asked. "For your information, Will does sometimes get paid for playing at the local clubs."

"Then why does he still live here with us?" Wanton asked.

"Because he doesn't make enough to move out on his own," Gloria replied.

"The bottom line is, our son needs to man up, and you need to stop treating him like a baby," Wanton exclaimed.

They heard footsteps on the porch and stopped talking. Will walked in, grabbed an uncut peach from the counter, took a bite, and kissed his mother on the cheek.

"Well, how are my two favorite parents doing today?" Will asked.

Wanton turned and looked at his son. "What the hell is that you've got on, boy?"

"Kinda fly, isn't it?" Will said, tugging at the collar of his jacket. "Want me to get you one?"

Wanton bellowed, "Boy, why can't you be like the rest of the guys your age? You're walking around here looking likc a damn clown!"

"Because I have to be me," Will replied. "Think about it, Dad. If everyone were the same, the world would be dull." Will walked off toward his bedroom.

"See what I mean, Gloria?" Wanton uttered. "I don't have time for this. I've got to get back to work." He kissed his wife and walked out.

"My God!" Gloria whispered in the quiet of the kitchen.

Pee Wee sat close to Bertha at the hamburger stand. He sat so close that whenever she turned sideways, he was dangerously close to her face. They shared a large heaping of fries. He watched as Bertha delicately dipped hers in ketchup, and the way she lifted them to her mouth.

"Why don't you put your horn down?" Bertha asked. "Isn't it uncomfortable trying to eat and hold that thing, too?"

"Are you crazy? I wouldn't dream of letting this trumpet out of my hands."

Bertha leaned back. She stared at him. "Well, excuse me."

"This," Pee Wee said, shaking his trumpet, "you don't understand. This is everything to me. Without it I'm nothing."

"Are you in a band or something?" Bertha asked.

"Honey," he replied with a grin, "I am the band."

Will walked into the kitchen that evening and was greeted with a familiar, sweet aroma. His stomach growled in response. His mother was bent over the oven, pulling out a long baking pan. He smiled, hungrily, taking off his jacket. "Mom, is that peach cobbler I smell?"

"It is," she said, casting a glance at him over her shoulder.

"Can I have a taste?" asked Will.

"You'll have to wait until after dinner.""Can I have just a little taste, Mom?" Will pleaded and pouted.

"Just a little taste," she agreed.

Will turned, grabbed a tablespoon and a bowl from the cabinet, and scooped up a generous helping of cobbler.

Gloria smacked the side of his head. "Boy, I said a taste, and here you go getting a bowl."

Holding tight to the bowl, Will sat down at the kitchen table. "Mom, you know I can't have just a little bit of your cobbler! It's too good." After sliding the first spoonful in his mouth, he tapped his foot against the floor.

Gloria walked over to him. "You okay?"

"Yeah, Mom. You outdid yourself this time! This cobbler must have been kissed by the angels above."

Gloria tapped the back of his head. "Boy, you say that same old thing all the time."

"This is the best cobbler."

She wiped her hands on her apron, a nervous habit of hers. She sat down across from her son. "Will, I wanted to talk to you about something while your father's not around. He's worried about you."

Will didn't look up from his bowl. "Why?" he asked.

Gloria paused. She knew she had to choose her words carefully because Will was sensitive to subjects involving his father. If she said the wrong thing, she would risk alienating him; it was bad enough he was barely speaking with his father. The relationship between Will and his father had become strangers as Will got older and began to understand the ills of society. Their relationship started to pull apart over disagreements about what was appropriate. They argued about the place of colored people and if they would ever enjoy all the freedoms other people enjoyed. Their arguments made Gloria weary and hopeful they would come to an agreement at some point, even if that agreement was to respectfully disagree. Gloria feared the men in her life were growing worlds apart.

"Your father and I had a talk about you today, and we agreed that you should get a job and be a bit more responsible," said Gloria. "You see, we love you and we will not always be around to provide for you."

"I know, Mom. What am I supposed to do? Join the army like Dad, or perhaps I could be a porter on a train; that is not what God put me here for."

"Enlighten me," Gloria replied. "Tell me. Why do you think God put you here? I am interested to know."

"Do you remember Professor Davis?" Will asked.

"Oh, Lord!" Gloria said. "Please don't tell me that you have been listening to that kook."

"Mom, he was not a kook. He was quite an intelligent man, and more than a teacher, he was like a father to me," Will expressed.

"I see now, the good doctor has corrupted your mind," Gloria replied.

"No, Mom. He has freed my mind, taught me to "Lift my Voice and Sing," taught me the "Freedom's Plow," gave me this guitar, and taught me the Word, and the Word is the truth," Will declared."You remember what happened to him, don't you?" avowed Gloria. "He was hauled off to one of those federal prisons and hasn't been seen since."

"Do you know why he was sent to prison?" Will asked. "I'll tell you why . . . because he stood for something. He stood for equality, justice, and fairness for all, and I am thankful that I had the honor of being one of his students. I hope that I can one day have an impact on someone's life like he has had upon mine."

"Well, I just hope you don't find yourself in prison, or even worse, strung up on somebody's tree for acting like someone that has given us so much," Gloria replied.

Disenchanted, Will shook his head in frustration and walked away.

Chapter Two

Whenever SFC Wanton wanted to blow off steam, he went to the noncommissioned officer's club, called the Eagle's Nest, a place where he could relax with colleagues. Though the army base had divisions other than race, the clubs were divided by ranks as well as race. Like the larger world around them, which assigned status to color and income, the military had its own caste system. Social interactions with others not of the same rank was expressly forbidden.

Although SFC Wanton understood the separation of ranks in the military, he didn't completely understand the separate but equal laws of Jim Crow anywhere, yet he never complained about them. He knew Lincoln's Gettysburg Address stated that all men are created equal, but he never questioned those who discriminated against his equal rights. He didn't join the military only because he loved his country; he joined to show his country that he was no different than any other American. He wanted to lead by example.

The Eagle's Nest served as a sanctuary for the black leaders in the army. There they could discuss the different things they would experience in their units, and ways to manipulate their white leaders into doing the things they wanted done.

19

For any colored man, it was an honor to have the rank of sergeant. The only thing that separated Wanton from most of his superiors, other than his color, was a degree from a historically black university, and a few more years' experience. He understood that the chances of colored men being field grade officers were slim to none, so he settled for the only opportunity the army gave him, and he was proud to have come as far as he had.

As he sat back on the barstool with a gin and juice in his hand, he thought about his life and the goals he'd had as a young man. He was proud to be able to say he'd reached every milestone he'd hoped for. He had married well, his career was on the trajectory he'd worked for, and his son was a young man, but not the man he wanted him to be, and that deeply disturbed him. Gloria, on the other hand, loved their son unconditionally. People on Wanton's side of town often complimented him because of his son's talent. Wanton knew his son was a talented musician, but he didn't think that playing instruments and singing could provide a future for his son. Wanton was deeply concerned that Will didn't take life seriously.

The thing that bothered Wanton most about his son Will was his propensity to go against the grain of society, speak up, and challenge authority. Will often complained about the system and how blacks would never be treated fairly if they did not stand up for their rights. Wanton, a religious man, believed that everything happened for a reason, and God sometimes allowed things to happen to strengthen our character. This was much like a parent disciplining a child to build his character. Wanton believed that our prayers aren't always answered when we want but in God's time. Therefore, Wanton believed the only way to get ahead was to play by the rules, exceed in every way possible, and eventually prayers would be answered, which was why Will believed his father was a victim of a colonized mind.

Wanton slowly sipped on his liquor and let the warmth of it spread through his chest, hoping that one day his son would see the world as he did and understand that he couldn't win a game of cards when the deck was stacked against him.

SFC Wanton was aware of a man slipping onto the barstool next to him but didn't look up right away. He felt a pat on his back and looked up.

"How are you doing there, Sarge?" SFC Richard said with a smile.

Wanton nodded. "It's been a day, I guess. Sometimes I just don't know."

"What's on your mind?" Richard asked.

"Beer, please," Wanton asked as the bartender strolled by. The man nodded and came back with an icy, frothy glass of brew. He took a sip before answering.

"It's my son," he said. "I worked hard to teach him how to be a man, how to take responsibility for himself. I honestly don't know what I could have done differently. My father taught me that a man should lead by example, and I did that, but somehow my son didn't get it. He is not remotely close to being the kind of man I wanted to see him grow up to be."

"Aww, hell man, that's normal," Richard said, patting him on the back. "Kids never do what we want them to, not without a fight anyway."

Chapter Three

Pee Wee and Bertha held hands while walking down the street later that afternoon. As they passed a store front, Pee Wee looked up and noticed a huge poster: a picture of Uncle Sam pointing an accusing finger and the words Uncle Sam Wants You!

Bertha caught him staring. Rubbing his arm, she leaned close to him. "Why don't you join the army?"

He stopped in his tracks. Looking Bertha in the eye, he smiled. "'Cause I'm a lover, baby, not a fighter," Pee Wee said, then gave a blast on his horn.Bertha nudged his shoulder. "You're crazy."

"Crazy about you," he replied as they continued to walk slowly down the street. Pee Wee enjoyed being close to her. "So, what kinds of things do you like?" he asked.

"Listening to music," Bertha said.

"Well, I like making music, so that makes us perfect for one another."

Bertha was quiet for a moment, but Pee Wee caught the smirk on her face. She was blushing, just enough to add rosiness to her brown skin. "What other things are you into?" she asked.

Pee Wee smiled. He hoisted himself up the stairs of a building. He went up three steps and looked down at Bertha. He touched her cheek. "You."

Her mouth opened in surprise. "What?" she whispered.

"I'm . . . into you."

He moved toward her and gave her a kiss right then and there.

In the early hours of the morning, soldiers were asleep in the barracks. All of a sudden, a steel garbage can flew through the air and bounced against the polished wooden floor, causing the men to jump out of their bunks. The lights came on. SFC Wanton walked in, calling out orders to his startled men.

"Get your asses up!" he hollered. "You have five minutes to get your physical fitness uniforms on and meet me outside; now move it!" Wanton exited.

The men jumped out of bed, putting on their pants and boots as fast as they could. Wanton walked outside and waited for the soldiers to come running out. They fell into formation and followed the orders he shouted out to them.

"You guys are dragging *ass* this morning!" he yelled. "Are you tired?"

"No, Sergeant!" they cried in unison.

"Now tell me the truth. If you are tired, let me know, and I will let you go back to bed. So, again. Are you tired?"

Wanton looked at his men. Some of them looked like they could barely keep their eyes open. Others frowned as if they might fall flat on their face from the concentration it took to stay awake.

"Yes, Sergeant," the men replied.

Wanton's face was expressionless. "On the command of 'fall out,' I will give you five minutes to get undressed and get into bed. Platoon! Attention!"

The soldiers snapped to attention.

"Fall out," Wanton ordered.

The soldiers couldn't believe their good luck. Some looked stunned that they were being allowed to go back inside, but none of them had to be told to follow this order twice.

"Sgt. Wanton is pretty cool," Johnson said.

"I know." Edwards grinned like a boy on Christmas morning. "I can't believe he's going to let us sleep in for the rest of the day."

Johnson looked around, lowering his voice to a whisper. "I can't either! I ain't mad at him." Wanton's boots echoed down the hall, and the men got nervous. "Quiet. Quiet. Here comes Sarge."

They had settled into their bunks, and at that moment they all closed their eyes and pretended to be asleep. There was complete silence as Wanton stalked through the barracks, not saying a word. He came to a stop in the middle of the room. The air was thick with tension, the soldiers afraid to breathe, speak, or even acknowledge the sergeant's presence.

Wanton yelled at the top of his lungs. "What in the hell do y'all think this is? This ain't no motherfucking motel. You get your sorry asses up out of bed right now!"

The soldiers jumped out of bed and dressed, confused and frightened. Some of them barely looked at each other; most got back into their clothes and stood at attention, afraid to meet the sergeant's eyes.

"Just in case you don't know, this is the Unites States Army, and American soldiers don't get tired. You have less than five minutes to get your lazy asses out in formation fully dressed and ready to work." With that, he turned and walked out of the barracks.

"What in the hell just happened?" Platt asked.

Later that morning Will decided to take a walk through the town. He ended up passing an army recruiting station. Curious, he stood outside with his hands in his pockets, watching the men who nervously awaited their physical exams. Some of the men were trying to get out of passing the physical fitness test. One man claimed his hearing was poor. A soldier leaned over and whispered in his ear. When the man didn't respond, the soldier crossed over to his other side and screamed in the man's ear. When the man jumped, the soldier shook his head and stamped the word PASS on his hearing exam with a big rubber stamp. He shoved the paper into the man's chest. It was obvious the man was disappointed to have been caught in a lie. "Next!" the soldier yelled.

Will shook his head and chuckled. Wow!

While looking through the window, he was startled when he saw the reflection of a beautiful young lady with caramel-colored skin standing behind him on the sidewalk. The reflection of the lady's body was angelic, to say the least. It was shaped like an hourglass and her skin golden and silky smooth. She wasn't quite white and not really black.

"Are you thinking about joining?" she asked. Measuring him with her wide brown eyes, she waited for an answer. She wore a pout on her full, red lips.

Turning to look at the girl, he mumbled, "For what?" He didn't mean for his reply to sound curt, but he didn't know this woman, and he had the feeling she was judging him in some way.

She wrinkled her brow. "To serve your country, of course."

"Really? What has this country done for me?"

"It's given you the opportunity to live as a free man."

Will gazed at her incredulously. "Apparently you don't know the meaning of freedom. Do you honestly think that you're free?"

"Sure, I can do whatever I want!" she replied.

Will shook his head. "That's sad. Look around you. Can't you see the signs?" he exuded. "You're bound by the rules of society, and you don't even know it." The girl was so used to seeing the separate but equal signs of Jim Crow, she was ignorant to their meaning. Another victim of the colonized mind.

In her Louisiana accent, she continued, "Babe, what do you expect? A society without any rules is lawless." "Well, you're just as confused as the people who are running this country. No man is truly free until he is master of himself." "You are one weird dude," the girl replied with one hand on her hip. "How could you not appreciate this great country of ours?" she asked as she stormed away.

Unable to let a stranger have the last word, Will called out to her, "Because we don't have the same rights as everyone in it!"

Pee Wee danced around in his kitchen, pressing the valves on his trumpet and occasionally stirring a pot of grits on the stove. He hummed, trying to work the kinks out of the melody to a new song he was trying to create. Once the grits were almost ready, he took a bowl down from the cabinet. Just as he was ready to pour them, he heard a knock at the door. Sighing, he put the pot down and went to answer the door, trumpet still in hand. When Pee Wee opened the door, Will walked right past him without even saying hello.

"Uh, so what's happening?" Pee Wee asked, shutting the door. He followed his friend back to the kitchen. Will pulled out a chair and sat down with a forlorn look on his face.

"How can our people not see the signs of bondage all around us? I mean, are we blind, or have we become numb to this type of treatment?" a frustrated Will asked.Pee Wee danced around with the pot of grits in one hand and his trumpet in the other; he poured some into a bowl. "Want some grits?" he asked.

"No thanks." Will grimaced.Pee Wee put the pot back on the stove, took the bowl, and sat at the table with Will, adding butter and sugar to his bowl.

Will jumped with excitement. "Oh man! I almost forgot to tell you. I met the most beautiful girl this morning. She's a common sense away from being perfect."

"What?" asked Pee Wee.

"She has everything but common sense.""Well, who is she?" Pee Wee asked.

"I don't know," Will replied.

Pee Wee burst into laughter. "What do you mean you don't know? You didn't even get the girl's name? Didn't you learn anything from me the other day? You may never see that girl again. I told you to take notes. See what happens when you don't listen to me?"

Will leaned back in his chair, lightly tapping the top of his guitar with his thumb, eyes downcast.

"This is exactly what I keep trying to tell you. You have to grab every opportunity when it presents itself," said Pee Wee. "She got under my skin when she said that I don't appreciate this is a free country," Will uttered. "Will, I have to ask: do you enjoy the freedoms this country has given to us?"

"No," Will replied. "Can you tell me one thing this country has done for black people?"

"Sure I can. This country abolished slavery and granted our people freedom a long time ago."

Will snickered. "So, you really think you are free? Well, I feel sorry for you because you only see what society wants you to see. It is true that we are no longer bound by chains; we're slaves to colonized minds." Will made his way toward the door.

Pee Wee leaned back in his chair. "Man, why are you so worried about that petty stuff?"

"It's those little inequities that bind our freedom," Will replied as he left.

SFC Wanton stood in front of the barracks counting the exhausted soldiers as they filed into formation. "You guys are still moving entirely too slow. So, we are going to do this until we get it right."

"This is bullshit," one of the soldiers whispered.

"What's that?" Wanton asked, spinning on his heel. "You think this is bullshit, Pvt. Jamal?"

"No, Sergeant!"

"That's right!" Wanton shouted as he walked back to the center of formation. "I'm going to tell you why. The enemy isn't going to wait until you get out of bed before he tries killing you. His goal is to take you out, whenever, wherever, and however he can. Therefore, you must be prepared at all times. So, on the command of 'fall out,' you will fall out and fall back into the barracks, and we will do this until I am satisfied."

Pee Wee and Will walked down the street talking about the girl of Will's dreams. "Will, you might as well forget about that girl. Chances are you'll never see her again," Pee Wee said. "Why don't you lighten up? I was hoping a walk would clear your mind."

"I am sorry, Pee Wee. Why am I talking about this girl anyway . . . there are more important things to talk about in this world like equality and justice," Will replied. "You know, it just frustrates me when I see the hypocrisy of this country and the way most of our people just accept it as if it is okay to be discriminated against and treated as second-class citizens." Pee Wee, being sarcastic, said, "Wow! What a relief, I thought you were upset about that girl."

"Some things are more important than self," explained Will.

Pee Wee snapped his finger. "Hey, I just had an idea that I am sure will brighten up your day."

"What's that?" Will asked.

"Bertha has a cousin visiting her from Louisiana. Why don't you let me introduce you to her?"

"Naw," Will said, staring at the sign across the street: Club 6661. He felt a strange sense of déjà vu. "I've seen this place, this sign before," he muttered.

"Well damn! You pass it every day," said Pee Wee. "Man, you are one weird dude. I love you, but you are weird as they come." Will, consumed by the sign, stated, "Pee Wee, I have to go and check out a few things."

"Are you coming to rehearsal tonight?" Pee Wee asked. Will nodded his head as he trotted across the street. "See you then." Pee Wee waved his trumpet above his head in acknowledgment as Will crossed the street.

Will stood on the corner, looking at the sign swinging in the breeze. He felt a lump form in his throat. What was it about this place that made him so uneasy? He did pass this spot almost every day, but the building was old and had been unattended for some time. The sign was what caught his attention—the club's name. He'd seen it in his dream. The sign swung on a rusty hinge, drawing further attention to itself. The thing that drew Will to the sign was that he always saw the latter part of the sign upside down in his dreams.

Unable to resist his curiosity, he entered the building. When he walked in, a bell sounded. It was nearly dark inside, except for the trail of light that came through the doorway. The club was covered with dust. Cobwebs hung from every corner.

"Hello," Will called. "Is anyone here?"

Will jumped when he felt a tap on his shoulder. He turned around to see a middle-aged white man with gray hair and a mustache.

"Who are you?" Will asked.

"My name's Peavy. I'm the owner. Still working on renovations, but we're hoping to get the place open next month. Are you looking for a job, son?"

"Uh, I have to go," Will said, and fled.

Peavy scratched his chin. "Weird," he muttered. Will ran back across the street and disappeared into the park. "I wonder if he could play that guitar. I need a good opening act."

Chapter Four

Field exercises went late into the evening. Wanton made them run through the routine until the men moved like a well-oiled machine. One soldier jumped from behind a log, waiting three seconds before dropping. He shot the moment he hit the ground. While he lay cover, his partner ran for another three seconds. The men repeated until they reached the bunker and simulated throwing a grenade.

SFC Wanton looked down at the soldier in the bunker, who was still poised to move if need be.

"Good job, soldier," Wanton said. He raised his hand and signaled for the troops to come out of hiding and rally around him. Just then, Captain Hicks walked up. Wanton called his men to attention and saluted the captain.

"At ease," the captain said. "Sergeant Wanton, can I speak with you for a moment?"

"Yes, sir." Wanton nodded and turned to Corporal Batts. "Corporal Batts, take over."

Once Hicks and Wanton were out of earshot, Captain Hicks put a finger to his lips. Wanton didn't show it, but he was already nervous to have the captain take him aside when he was in the middle of training. Usually when Hicks did come down, it was to have a look at how the men were doing. He couldn't remember a single time when the captain would interrupt him during training for a talk.

"You know, Sergeant, you're one of the finest soldiers I have ever had the pleasure of working with," explained Hicks.

"Thank you, sir. It means a lot coming from someone with your military knowledge," Wanton replied.

Hicks nodded. As they continued to walk, Wanton took in a quick breath, putting his arms behind his back.

"Right now, I'm having a problem I need you to help me with," said Hicks.

"Sir, just tell me what you'd like me to do," Wanton replied. "I am here to carry out your orders, sir."

"Well, it's your son, Will.""Will . . . What has that boy done now? That boy! I'll kill him," Wanton replied angrily.

"Hold on now, Sergeant." Hicks put a hand on his shoulder. "The boy just needs a little guidance. I'm asking you to take control of the situation."

"Sir, what exactly is he doing?"

Hicks let his hand fall away from Wanton's shoulder, clasping his hands in front of him while rolling back on his heels. "I'm told he's part of a Communist party that is forming in your community."

"Consider the actions of my son taken care of, sir."Captain Hicks began to walk away. He stopped for a moment, looking back at Wanton.

"Sergeant?"

"Yes, sir?"

"Don't let your son's actions destroy the career you've worked so hard for with his foolish actions of protesting against this fine country that you have served with great dignity."

Gloria was in the kitchen frying chicken as she hummed along to the melody Will played on his guitar. Will generally practiced at home during the day while his father was working, because his father complained about the noise of the guitar. She wished that weren't the case because she loved to hear Will strum on the guitar that Dr. Davis gave him. She beamed as she noticed the progress he had made. The melodies flowed smoothly, the chord progressions increasingly more precise. Though she'd only learned a bit of the technical language from him, she knew his music soothed both her ears and her heart.

She had just put the last piece of chicken into the frying pan and was wiping the counter when her husband came storming into the kitchen, slamming the door behind him.

"Where is he?" Bill shouted at Gloria.

The music in the other room abruptly ended with a sour note.

"In his room . . . honey, what's wrong?" she asked.

Will walked into the kitchen. "Dad . . . ?"

Yelling furiously, Wanton pointed a trembling finger at his son. "Boy, what in the hell do you think you are doing? Don't you realize all of your actions are a reflection on me?" Wanton shouted.

"What are you talking about?" Will inquired.

"You and your friends," Wanton hissed. "Hanging out in that damn park with those hippies, smoking dope and stirring up trouble."

"What?" Will questioned.

"This shit has got to stop!" he screamed. "From this day forward you are forbidden from hanging out with those troublemakers."

"I'm not one of your soldiers, and you can't tell me what to do!" Wanton shoved Will against the wall.

"Bill!" Gloria cried.

"Listen here, boy," he continued, ignoring his wife. "You're my damn son, and as long as you live in this house, you'll do what I say!"

Gloria grabbed her husband's shoulder, gently tugging at him so he'd let go of their son. Wanton released Will.

Without a word, Will grabbed his guitar and headed out the door.

"Where do you think you're going?" Wanton shouted

"Let him go, Bill. Don't make it worse by going after him," Gloria pleaded.

"What the hell is wrong with that boy?" Wanton asked.

Gloria threw her dish towel into the sink. She lowered the fire beneath the pan on the stove. "I think he has been influenced by Dr. Davis." Wanton stood silently with his hand over his lip for a moment. "I'll be damned, that explains a lot. That goofy-ass doctor has corrupted my son by feeding him all his anti-American rhetoric."

Will had nowhere in particular to go. Walking with his guitar strapped to his back, he found a park bench beneath a tree. The night was pleasantly warm. He began to play, letting his irritation melt beneath the movement of his fingertips. He was so into his music that he didn't hear anyone approach him. He nearly jumped when he felt a hand touch his shoulder.

He turned to see an elderly man standing over him. Though most of the man's face was hidden in the darkness of the night, Will could see the man was disfigured. Will also noticed the man proudly wore an old WWI uniform.

"You play that thing pretty well," the man said. "How long have you been playing?"

"Since I was fourteen. I had a professor who taught me basically everything I know before they took him off for encouraging people to stand up for equal rights," he replied. "He gave me this guitar because he said I had a special gift."

The man smiled and extended his hand to Will. "People call me Big Sarge."

Will shook his hand. "I'm Will, named after my father, unfortunately."

Big Sarge sat down with a sigh. He folded his hands into his lap and gave Will a quizzical look. "What brings you out here this late at night?"

"My father. He thinks I'm hurting his career by encouraging people to stand up for our equal rights.""Well, we all have our own crosses that we must bear; some are easier than others," Big Sarge explained.

"I guess you are right."Big Sarge motioned toward his guitar. "May I?"

"Sure." Will removed the guitar sling from around his neck and gave the guitar to Big Sarge.

Big Sarge took the guitar and started tuning it. "You know, I used to love this country with all my heart until I became disfigured during the war. Then I realized this country didn't give a damn about me. After nearly dying for this country, I am still being treated as a second-class citizen, and I understand your frustration with many of our people, as well as with your father."

"You know, you kind of remind me of Dr. Davis. He was a very educated man who tried to open our eyes to the injustices in this country.""Have you ever heard the song 'Lift Every Voice and Sing'?" asked Big Sarge.

"Yes, I have," replied Will. "Dr. Davis used to have us sing it every day before class."

"You know, that song is considered the black national anthem. I really didn't understand it until after the second big one."

"You were in World War I?" Will asked.

"Yes, I had a wife and son before the army took me off; haven't seen them since I have been back," said Big Sarge in a somber manner.

"How could you leave your family and give your life for a country that doesn't respect you as a man?" asked Will.

"It's very easy, son," said Big Sarge as he strummed the guitar, playing the melody of "May Freedom Reign." Big Sarge suddenly stopped strumming, looked at Will, and said, "It's about survival. We as men sometimes must do things that we may not like. You see, I joined the army as a means to support my family. For over twenty years I sent half my check to my wife and son so they would not starve."

"That's was very noble of you," said Will. "I bet your son really looks up to you."

"I have not seen him since I left for the war," said Big Sarge in a somber voice.

"But why?" asked Will. "I just couldn't let them see me in this way. As you can tell, my face was severely disfigured during the war," he said, motioning toward his face.

"Wow, that must be rough, to have a son that you can't even communicate with," said Will.

"How do you think your father feels?" asked Big Sarge. "Listen to these words I tell you: let no problem get too big between you and your father that you can't solve together, for we only have one life to live, therefore we should live it loving one another." Big Sarge gave Will's guitar back to him and faded back into the darkness of the night.

Will wasn't looking forward to going home that night, but he didn't have a choice. He could have stayed over at Pee Wee's if push really came to shove, but he didn't want to impose. The worst part of it was that he didn't know how long his dad was going to be mad at him. They'd had arguments before, but he couldn't remember seeing his old man that upset, ever.

When he arrived at the doorstep, Will knew what he was in for. He could see his parents in the kitchen, by the light above the stove. His mother sat at the table while his father paced the floor. Rather than going in through the kitchen door, Will went around and tried to sneak in through the front door without his father noticing him.

The moment Will crossed the threshold, he heard his father screaming. Rather than wait for his father to come into the living room, he went into the kitchen. He stood just inside the doorway, in the exact same spot he'd been in earlier that evening.

"Boy, where in the hell have you been?"

Will stood in silence and smiled.

"What the hell are you smiling at? Boy, don't you know you had your mother worried to death?"

"I love you too, Dad."

Will's father stood there, frustrated. Those four words had taken all the sting out of his righteous fury, and they both knew it. Instead of saying anything else, Wanton walked out of the kitchen.

"Love you, Mom," said Will as he walked over to her and kissed her on the cheek.

"What was that for?" Gloria asked.

"For being a wonderful mom," he said, and walked off to his bedroom.

The next morning, the soldiers jumped from their bunks as Sergeant Wanton walked down the corridor of their sleeping quarters yelling, "Get your asses up! The enemy doesn't wait for you to wake to attack! He wants to kill you while you sleep! It's easier that way!"

"Damn, it's three o'clock," one soldier whispered.

"Man," the soldier nearest him muttered, "his wife must be holding out on him."

"PT formation in five minutes!"

Wanton walked out of the barracks as soldiers ran past him to get into formation. They marched under his orders, and they ran as Wanton sang cadence.

Later that morning, Gloria said, "You know, Will, your father loves you."

Will nodded as his mother placed a bowl of oatmeal in front of him. She poured a cup of coffee for herself and sat down. Now Will's father was out of the house, he knew he was in for a talk from his mom. He simply nodded in agreement and let her enjoy her coffee for a minute. He needed to say something, but he knew she wasn't going to like it.

"Mom, the army is using people like Dad to keep us enslaved to the system, don't you think? I mean, they may allow one or two-colored people to get ahead but keep the rest of us down," he continued. "It's like pulling wool over our eyes."

"Honey, you don't understand. Your father is in a very complex situation. On one hand, he is protecting the interest of a nation that denies him equality, but on the other hand, he is providing his family with a comfortable life. So, tell me, what would you have him do?"

Will rubbed his head and sighed, leaning back in his chair.

"I don't know, Ma." Will rested his elbows on the edge of the table. "It's a dilemma. Dad's a soldier and we are guaranteed the right to free speech by the United States Constitution. Yet we're suppressed from using it. So, I ask, do we stand up and speak out against racial inequality, or do we allow ourselves to continue to be suppressed by maintaining our silence? What would you have me do?" Will begged of her.

"Honey, just work with your dad a little? After all, he's fighting to make this country a better place for you and me."

Will straightened his back and looked at his Mom. "Mom, someone has to take a stand."

Gloria replied, "That someone doesn't have to be you."

"If not me, then who?" "I don't care who. I am not willing to sacrifice my only son for a change in society," said Gloria.

"You believe in God, don't you?" "Of course I do," Gloria said.

"Then you must know that God has a purpose for all of us.""God didn't bring you to life just to get killed for protesting against the government.""God didn't bring Jesus into the world just to follow unjust laws made by man, either," Will replied.

"Well okay, genius, then why did God send Jesus to the world?" Gloria asked."To die for our sins. It's in the Word, John 3:16," Will replied as he walked toward the door. He stopped in the doorway to look back at his mother. "Work without deeds is dead." He left the house.

Wanton ordered his men to shower and prepare the barracks for inspection. The moment he got inside, Pvt. Jamal collapsed onto his bunk.

"Come on, man, we have to get ready for inspection," Pvt. Platt said. He reached over and tapped Jamal on the leg.

"Man, this shit is for the birds," he groaned.

"Would you rather be in jail?" Platt asked.

Jamal jumped up and grabbed a towel from his wall locker. Platt sat on his bed, staring, surprised at his friend's sudden burst of energy.

"What are you sitting around for, man?" Jamal said. "We have things to do."

Platt smiled and shook his head. He started making his bed while Jamal headed off toward the showers.

The park was a hotbed of activity that afternoon. There was a group on stage performing, and the crowd was into it. Many of the students held up anti–Jim Crow signs: I Am Man. The crowd loved the performers, and the energy they gave the day was electrifying.

Will walked up to Pee Wee, who sat on the edge of the stage.

Pee Wee twirled his trumpet. "Hey, man, we were supposed to meet here an hour ago. What are we going to do? These guys playing are hot." Will nodded. "This is not a competition. Music is merely food for the soul." "Well, I hope people are still hungry by the time that group finishes," Pee Wee replied.

The other guys in their band had gathered around, and there was a general grumble of consensus with Pee Wee.

"Come on," Will said. "Circle of love."

They gathered in a huddle and recited the Lord's Prayer.

Pressing the valves on his trumpet, Pee Wee looked up when the prayer was over. "All right. Let's do this."

They took the stage, each man behind his instrument, and Will at the mic with his guitar. The drummer sat in the background as Will looked out over the audience. He began the intro to their song with a speech.

"A man once said, 'A house divided against itself cannot stand.' I want to tell you today that *equality* is the bridge that can bring our houses together . . . and to form a more perfect union we must put an end to Jim Crow and the concept of separate but equal." Will played a couple of riffs on his guitar, the band joined in, and the crowd went wild.

"Saying separate but equal is like saying different but the same."

People began to dance and move in time with the music as the band played. Some sang along, and others swayed with the rhythm. Will looked across the audience and saw Mr. Peavy, the owner of Club 6661. Bertha walked past him, guiding another girl with her through the crowd.

Will stopped.

Right in the middle of a song, he couldn't move. The girl beside Bertha was the same one he'd met in front of the army recruitment office.

Pee Wee snatched the mic and started singing, picking up where Will left off as if the whole thing were planned. The audience cheered—no one seemed to realize anything was wrong, but Will stood there love struck. Pee Wee bumped Will, bringing him out of his trance long enough to sing the last few lines of the song.

"I told you," Bertha said, nudging her cousin's arm. "That's my baby up there!"

Karen frowned. Bertha grabbed her arm, and the two of them navigated through the crowd toward the stage. When they got there, Bertha jumped into Pee Wee's arms and kissed his cheek. "You were great! I didn't know you could play like that."

"You better recognize!" Pee Wee replied.

Will walked up just then.

"Hey, let me introduce you to my best friend, Will. Will, this is my girl's cousin, Karen, the girl I was telling you about."

Will stepped up to Karen and smiled. "All this time I thought angels were in heaven . . ."

"Excuse me?" Karen interrupted him. Her lip curled upward in distaste.

"But here you are right here on earth," Will said.

Karen shook her head and folded her arms over her chest. "Is that the best line you can come up with? Because I'm not impressed."

"Am I supposed to say things to impress you?" Will asked.

Pee Wee looked at Bertha then at Will. "Do you two know each other?"

"We had a brief encounter," Will said coolly.

"Oh, that's nice. Maybe we could double date," Bertha suggested.

"Not a chance, baby," Karen replied.

Will felt someone slap his shoulder, and he almost jumped. He turned to see Mr. Peavy. "You guys were great," he said to the boys. "You sound incredible."

"Thanks." Pee Wee grinned proudly and spun his trumpet for emphasis.

"My name is Mr. Peavy," he said, extending his hand to both musicians. "I'm the owner of the club down the street. You guys are something special."

"You mean the new club that is opening this weekend?" Pee Wee asked.

"That would be the one," Peavy replied. "I'm also an executive at Revival Records."

"Hot damn," Pee Wee said.

"I was wondering if you guys would be interested in signing with us and playing a couple gigs down at the club," Peavy offered.

Will answered quickly, "No thanks."

Pee Wee looked at his partner in disbelief as Will walked away. "Don't worry about him," Pee Wee turned to Mr. Peavy. "Hell, I'll sign."

"Sorry, son. It's an all-or-nothing deal," Peavy explained. "Here's my number. Give me a call when you guys get it together and want to make some money."

"Consider us part of your company, because we're going to sign. You can believe that," Pee Wee assured him.

Peavy nodded politely and walked away.

Pee Wee tucked the business card into his pocket and gave Bertha a squeeze. "Did you hear that, baby? I'm going to be a star."

"Not without the rebel," she said, gesturing in Will's direction.

"He's going to sign, one way or the other," Pee Wee said. "Bertha, can I talk to you later? I've got to go talk some sense into Will."

"Good luck with that!" shrieked Karen.

"I'm so proud of my man," Bertha said. "An honest to goodness musician, hot damn!"

Karen, puzzled by what had just happened, kept her silence.

Will was more than a block away by the time Pee Wee caught up with him.

"Hey, wait up, man!" Pee Wee yelled. Will turned and waited for him. They fell into step on the sidewalk. Will moped, hands in his pockets, eyes averted from his friend.

"What's wrong with you, man?" Pee Wee asked.

Will waited a moment before answering. "You don't understand, Pee Wee. If we sign a contract, he owns us."

"So what? I'll be a rich-ass slave!" Pee Wee replied.

"Pee Wee, there's more to life than money," Will countered. "If we sign a contract, we will be giving away the little freedom we have."

"Will, if you don't have a goal, you are bound to hit it. Do you remember when you told me about a girl you met a couple days ago but didn't get her number or her name?"

"What's that have to do with this?" Will asked.

"Everything. It's about seizing the moment. Capitalizing on opportunities. If you don't aim at anything, then you will not hit anything," Pee Wee implored.

"Is that contract worth selling your soul?" Will asked. "'Cause I'm not for sale."

Will turned to walk away, but Pee Wee caught his arm. "Man, at least think about it."

Will nodded. "Okay, but I am ninety-nine-point nine percent sure that I will not change my mind."

Chapter Five

SFC Wanton walked into Captain Hicks's office. Another officer was already seated with him, and Wanton saluted him. "Sir, Sergeant Wanton reports, sir."

"At ease, have a seat, Sergeant," said Hicks. Wanton sat at the seat in front of Hicks's desk. "What can I do for you, Sergeant?" asked Hicks.

"Sir, I wrote a memorandum to see if we could get the range for marksmanship training."

"Oh." Hicks snapped his fingers. "I almost forgot. The range will not be available for a while."

Wanton remained still, trying not to reveal any emotion. He kept his voice level and modulated. "Sir, given the current situation, my men need the training. If given the call, I want my men to be ready."

"Thank you for reminding me about the range, but I will no longer be handling the training. Our new platoon leader Lieutenant Dukes will schedule training from now on."

Wanton looked over at the lieutenant and extended his hand for a handshake. Dukes waved him away.

"There's no need to be all formal," Dukes said. "I heard a lot about you, boy."

Wanton stared at him, clearly not pleased about being called "boy" or the fact that this man refused even a simple handshake. Instead of addressing it, he snapped into attention, regarding Captain Hicks and ignoring Dukes.

"Sir, if you have no further business, I would like to get back to my troops," Wanton retorted.

"Carry on, Sergeant," Hicks said.

Once Wanton was gone, Dukes turned to Hicks. "Captain, I would like to look at my new troops."

Hicks stood. "Well, if you'll give me a few minutes, I'll take you over to the barracks to see your platoon."

Wanton's men stood in formation, waiting for the sergeant to inspect their barracks. They'd spent most of the day cleaning and scrubbing, hoping to pass muster. They were quiet as the moments passed, while Wanton was inside, checking their work. The sergeant kicked the screen door open and came outside to face them.

"Your living quarters look like shit. You are an embarrassment to the United States Army. Does anyone know why your barracks look like shit?"

"No, Sergeant!"

"I'll tell you why. I have failed you! I've been taking it too easy on you. From this day forward, I will be where you are. I will be deeper into you than the air you breathe. You remember that weekend pass you were going to get this weekend? You can forget it. Your weekend will be spent right here cleaning your quarters." Wanton scowled.

Lieutenant Dukes and Captain Hicks walked up along the side of the formation. Dukes stopped and looked at the men, hands behind his back, before turning to address Wanton.

"Sergeant Wanton, are my troops ready for inspection?"

"No, sir!" Wanton replied.

Dukes stepped up to Wanton, close enough that their faces were inches from each other. "Why aren't my troops ready, Sergeant? I'll tell you why, it's because *you* failed them. That's why you will spend this weekend writing a report to me on why my troops aren't prepared for inspection."

Wanton rolled backward on his heels. He bit down on his bottom lip, clenching his hands into fists. Dukes turned toward the soldiers and addressed them. "As for you troops, while your platoon sergeant is writing out his report, I want you to enjoy this weekend pass."

The entire platoon erupted with cheers of joy. Wanton gave them a stern look and they snapped back to attention. He turned and walked down toward the street without a word, shoulders raised and shoes echoing against the sidewalk.

Will stood in a field of dandelions, blowing on them to see how they gently flew through the breeze, enjoying the moments of freedom he gave them. Feeling the sensation that he was being watched, he turned around and found Karen standing behind him.

"What are you doing here?" Will asked.

"This is a free country, isn't it?" she replied sarcastically.

"That depends on who you ask.""Well, I'm asking you."Will thought long and hard. Without saying a word, he walked up to Karen, grabbed her by the arms, and tried to kiss her. She pulled back and slapped him. Staring at her in shocked silence, Will rubbed his face. She was so angry that he could feel the heat coming from her body. Her face was red. "Guess what? Your freedom ends where mine begins," Karen said with assurance.

"What's wrong with you, Jamal? We get a taste of freedom tonight and you look like you lost your best friend," asked Platt as he jumped down from his bunk and looked over at his friend, who was half dressed but getting ready slowly, as if he dreaded it. The rest of the soldiers in the barracks were happily chatting and preparing for their night off base.

"I don't know," Jamal said. "Something just ain't right."

"Did you see the way our new platoon leader clowned Sergeant Wanton?" Platt said. A soldier walking past them overheard them and shook his head in agreement.

"Yes, but . . . ," Jamal said.

"I thought you said you didn't like Sgt. Wanton," Platt prodded.

"It's our new platoon leader," Jamal lowered his voice. "I just don't like the way he clowned Wanton in front of us."

Platt patted him on the back. "I tell you what, you can sit here thinking all weekend if you want. But I'm going to make the best of my weekend pass with some super fine women."

Corporal Batts walked over to Jamal's bunk. "What's wrong? Are you afraid that everyone is going to see that you are all mouth?"

Jamal jumped from his bed, walked to his wall locker, and put on his class A shirt. "Platt, let's go teach these boys something."

Batts passed Preacher's bunk and stopped. "Hey, Preach, aren't you coming?"

The soldier lay on his bunk with his Bible open.

"Naw," he said softly. "Ain't nothing out there for me."

Jamal looked shocked. "What do you mean ain't nothing out there for you? The place is going to be full of beautiful single women."

Preacher shrugged. "That's all fine and dandy, but when the Lord wants me to have a woman, he will send me one."

"Why wait for the Lord?" Jamal asked. "I can get you a woman tonight."

"Thanks, but I'll pass," Preacher said.

"Okay, suit yourself," Jamal replied, straightening his shirt. "Just means more for me."

Club 6661 was having its grand opening, and it was packed. Seven soldiers entered the club together. The girls were certainly giving them all their attention. The local men were getting jealous because it was hard to compete with fine, muscled young men in uniform.

"Women do like these uniforms," Platt said with a grin.

"Mama always told me women like men in uniform," Doc teased.

"I've never seen so many beautiful women in one place in my life."

Professor nodded, scanning the crowd. "They're beautiful, too. Preach doesn't know what he's missing."

Platt spoke up. "So, what are you guys going to do? Sit around and talk about Preach all night or go get some?"

"We're going to play a couple games of pool and have a few drinks at the bar, and then we will show you guys how to get some girls," said the professor as he led some of the men toward the bar.

"Yeah, right," Platt replied as he signaled to Jamal and pointed to two beautiful women sitting alone at a table. The two of them walked over to the two girls and asked them to dance. The girls both smiled and walked onto the dance floor with the men.

The soldiers walked past the table where Will and Pee Wee sat together. Will shook his head. "I feel sorry for those poor, misguided souls."

"What do you have against those guys?" Pee Wee asked. He was playing with his trumpet, his fingers moving absently over the valves but not pressing down. He could hold a conversation and outline the notes to a new song in his mind without missing a word of what was going on around him.

"Nothing," Will said. "Look at them. They think they own the place."

Just then, Bertha and Karen walked into the club. The moment she saw Will, Karen turned to leave. Bertha grabbed Karen's arm and dragged her cousin halfway to the table.

"Oh boy," Will sighed, putting a hand over his face.

"Hey, baby," Bertha said, leaning over to kiss Pee Wee.

Karen sat down in the farthest corner of the table away from Will.

"What are you doing here?" Will snarled.

Karen smirked at Will and put a hand to her jaw. "Oh, I just came to show my face. Bertha, can you believe it? This place has real men in it, too," she said, pointing toward the soldiers.

Will mimicked Karen while her back was turned, and Pee Wee choked back a laugh. "Let's not forget," Will said, "clothes don't make a man. It's a man who makes the clothes."

Pee Wee shook his head. "Bertha, baby, are you ready to show me some more of your moves?"

The two of them disappeared onto the dance floor, leaving Will and Karen alone.

"Do you mind if we?" Will asked, pointing at the dance floor.

"As a matter of fact, I do," Karen shot back. She got up and went to get a drink from the bar. As she walked past a group of soldiers, Pvt. Kennedy grabbed her rear and squeezed her. Not knowing which of the guys had touched her, she slapped Pvt. Johnson, the soldier nearest to her.

"Bitch! Are you out of your motherfuckin' mind?" Johnson shouted.

"Who the hell do you think you are?" Karen yelled back.

Will smiled, folded his arms, and turned his chair to watch the show.

Pee Wee and Bertha made their way through the crowd to save her.

Pee Wee stepped between Karen and Pvt. Johnson. "Hold on, man, what's going on here?"

"This bitch slapped me!"

"Oh no, who you think you calling a bitch? Bitch!" Bertha said.

Pee Wee moved both girls behind him. "I'll handle this."

Batts, Jamal, and Platt left the dance floor.

"Look, you need to mind your own business before I stomp a mud hole in your little ass," Johnson snarled.

Batts and Jamal pushed Johnson away gently, trying to calm the situation.

Will walked up to the commotion. "What good will it do for you, a US soldier, to fight the very people that you were trained and sworn to protect?" Everyone turned to look at Will, who stood there calmly.

Batts nodded. "He's right, you know."

Jamal spoke up. "Look, we just got this pass and we don't need to give them an excuse not to give us another one."

Corporal Batts and the soldiers went to one corner; Pee Wee, Will, Bertha, and Karen went back to their table.

The soldiers gathered around Batts. "What in the hell just happened?" asked Batts.

Pvt. Kennedy tried to hide his smile. "All I know is that girl slapped the liquor out of Johnson."

Batts noticed Kennedy trying to hide his laughter, avoiding eye contact. He turned to Pvt. Johnson. "What happened?" Batts asked.

Johnson shook his head. "Hell, I don't know. The only thing that I know is that girl slapped me, talking 'bout how I grabbed her on the butt."

"Well, did you?" Batts asked.

"Naw, I didn't," Johnson said.

Batts sighed. "Okay, okay, fellas, let's try to stay out of trouble for once."

Will ordered a round of drinks for their table. Pee Wee turned to Karen. "You can't go around slapping people like that."

"Baby, that guy grabbed her butt," Bertha said. "What was she supposed to do?"

"I'm just saying," Pee Wee said. "Karen, you just have to be careful not to let yourself get put into a compromising position."

"Yeah," Will added. "That temper of yours can get you dealt with around here."

Karen rolled her eyes.

"Hey," Pee Wee said, pointing at Karen, "stay out of trouble. Now baby, let's go back and finish doing our thing." Pee Wee led Bertha back to the dance floor.

Will waited until his friends were out of earshot before leaning over and mocking Karen. "You know, I JUST LOVE men in uniform."

"Shut up, you jerk!" Karen screeched.

On the opposite end of the club, the soldiers were playing pool and having more drinks. Kennedy stood watching Johnson as he attempted to hit a ball into the corner pocket.

"Man, that girl slapped you so hard I fell down," Kennedy said. "Look at you! I bet her handprint is still on your face." The soldiers laughed at Johnson.

Humiliated, Johnson sunk the ball in the pocket. Standing up slowly, he looked at Kennedy. "Shut up, punk, before I leave my handprint on your face."

"Hey, look here, baby, don't get mad at me. I am not the one that slapped you. Look at her over there with her man," Kennedy continued.

"If she wasn't a woman, I would beat her like she stole something," Johnson seethed.

"Well, there's her man," Kennedy said.

Johnson took a long gulp of beer. "I ought to beat him down."

"Now you're talking," Kennedy said. "That's what I would do."

Johnson got up and strolled toward Will and Karen's table, with other soldiers behind him. As the men approached, Will couldn't help but comment to Karen, "Look, it's your boyfriend; he's coming over."

Will was about to ask the soldiers what they wanted, but he never got the chance. Johnson sucker punched him square in the jaw, sending him to the floor. Pee Wee saw his friend go down. He jumped on a table and straight onto Johnson's back. Pee Wee's friends and the rest of the band jumped in, grabbing any soldier they could.

Batts saw the commotion. "Damn it!" He broke away from his table along with Platt and Jamal, attempting to intervene and break up the fight, but it was out of control. Within minutes the police rushed through the door and arrested all the soldiers and civilians involved in the fight.

Pee Wee struggled as he was handcuffed and they tried to take his horn away.

"Hey!" he screamed. "Give that back!"

Chapter Six

Will was in a cell with the rest of his band; the soldiers were crammed into the cell next to them. Will sprang up from his seat and looked through the bars, as if he expected to see someone coming their way soon.

"My dad is going to kill me," Will groaned.

"Will, your father doesn't have to know," Pee Wee said. "Damn, I can't believe they took my baby."

"Pee Wee, damn that horn, tell me how we are supposed to get out of here?" Will bellowed. He sat down in the seat, crossing his arms over his chest.

"Don't worry," Pee Wee said. "I got that covered. My Bertha is going to get the money to bail us out."

In the cell next to them, Corporal Batts paced back and forth. The soldiers were all silent, eyes downcast.

"Well, you guys can kiss the chances of us getting any more passes good-bye," Corporal Batts said.

"Damn, Johnson, why in the hell did you have to start a fight?" Platt asked.

"You just messed everything up," Jamal added. "Damn!"

Just then, Captain Hicks and SFC Wanton burst into the jailhouse. Wanton went to the desk where the jailer sat, while Hicks turned toward Batts and spoke to him through the cell's bars."What can I do for you, boy?" the jailer asked Wanton.

"I came to see if you would release those soldiers into my custody," Wanton replied.

"Under whose authority should I release these soldiers?"

Wanton stood tall. "By the authority given to me by the United States Army."

The jailer chuckled. "Son, I don't know what you think this is, but coloreds have no authority in my jailhouse."

Captain Hicks bristled. Red faced, he turned to the jailer. "Who in the hell do you think you are? This man is a soldier in the United States Army. These stripes are all the authority he needs, and you will give him the same respect that you give me."

"Well, sir, I . . . I didn't mean any harm."

"Whether you meant it or not, you disrespected this soldier. Here is a man willing to put his life on the line to protect the freedoms that *your sorry ass* enjoys, that alone commands respect; color should be a nonissue. I highly suggest that you release these people into his custody. Or do I need to call your chief?"

"Sir, that won't be necessary."

"Good," Captain Hicks said, and walked out of the building.

Wanton crossed his arms and grinned at the man. "I guess you'd better get started on that paperwork."

"Yes, sir. If you would give me a moment, I will have those soldiers released into your custody quicker than you can blink an eye."

Wanton walked over to the cell and looked at his men. "I hope you enjoyed your pass this weekend, 'cause you won't see another one for a long time."

"That's right!" Pee Wee said, staring them down.Wanton looked over to the adjoining cell. "Pee Wee?" he said in surprise. It only took him a moment to notice Will sitting to his left. "Boy, what in the hell are you doing here? Hold on. I'll deal with you later."

"Pee Wee, you just had to open your big mouth, huh?" Will sighed.

Wanton approached the jailer. "Excuse me, sir. Since my boys caused this disturbance, I would like you to release the rest of the people involved."

"Well, I don't know if I can do that," said the jailer.

"Maybe the captain could convince you," Wanton commented as he walked toward the door.

"Hold on, Sarge," the jailer replied. "That won't be necessary. I suppose I can make an exception this time."

"So, you will release them all?" Wanton asked.

"Yes."

Walking back over to the cell, Wanton addressed his son and his friends. "As soon as they let you out, take your asses home. No detours, no exceptions . . . and I'll deal with you later," he said, pointing at Will.

"Sir," the jailer called, "if you sign here, I'll release the soldiers into your custody."

Wanton signed, and the jailer released the soldiers and the local boys that were fighting with them.

"Corporal Batts," he said, "take the soldiers back to the barracks and have them in their BDUs at 0500 hrs. Also tell Captain Hicks that I will be there as soon as possible, because I have to finish some paperwork here."

"Yes, Sergeant."

"All right, I need one more signature," the jailer said, indicating where the sergeant should sign. Once he reviewed the paperwork, the man opened the door so the band members could leave.

"Thank you, Mr. Wanton," Pee Wee said.

Will was the last person to leave the cell. Wanton looked at his son in disappointment as Will walked past him.

Bertha and Karen walked into the jailhouse together. "Honey, I've got your bail!" Bertha called out.

"It's okay. Will's dad just got us out," Pee Wee explained.

Karen walked over to Will and put both hands on his face. "I'm so sorry all this happened," she said.

Wanton looked at the girl and the expression on his son's face, and smiled. In that moment, he saw Will as a chip off the old block and beamed with pride.

Preach sat alone in the barracks, still reading his Bible, using the light from his flashlight. The door opened and disturbed the quiet peace Preacher was having with the Lord. His fellow soldiers walked back in to the living quarters, most of them looking like their puppy had just died.

"Once and for all," Batts asked. "Will somebody tell me what the fuck happened?"

Preach sat up, perplexed. The men were silent.

"I'll tell you what happened," Kennedy offered, laughing. "Johnson here got slapped silly by some girl in the club." Batts turned to Johnson. "What happened, Johnson?"

"I don't know. Some woman said that I grabbed her behind, then she slapped me," explained Johnson.

"Well, did you?" asked Batts.

"No, it wasn't me, boss," Johnson said.

"Well, if you didn't," Jamal asked, "who did?"

Pvt. Johnson shrugged. "I don't know."

"Who was standing next to you?" Professor asked.

All the soldiers turned to look at Pvt. Kennedy. Johnson slapped Kennedy so hard that he fell to the floor. Johnson picked Kennedy up by the collar and shook him. The guys surrounded them as Johnson landed another solid punch. Preach jumped out of his bunk and got dressed so he could go see what was happening.

"You're the one that caused all of this trouble!" Johnson said, shaking Kennedy.

"Get him, beat his ass!" one of the soldiers yelled. "He messed up my weekend!" cried another.

Wanton walked in.

"At ease!" Batts cried.

The soldiers backed off. Johnson and Kennedy got up and stood at attention in the sergeant's presence.

"What the hell is going on?" Wanton screamed. "You guys not only disgraced yourselves; you disgraced your race and the United States Army."

The soldiers looked out the corner of their eyes toward Pvt. Kennedy. He stared straight ahead, pretending he didn't feel their anger. He bit down on his lower lip, clutching his hands behind his back.

SFC Wanton walked to the end of the corridor and grabbed a chair. He dragged it to the center of the floor and sat down. "Bring it in, sit down, or take a knee."

Some sat, others kneeled, but they all gathered around Wanton in a semicircle. Wanton removed his hat and scratched his head. "Guys, I want you to realize how important your role is in society. You are representatives of the United States Army. More importantly, you represent your race. The things that you do are a direct reflection upon every black American in the United States. For us to get recognition as average soldiers, we must be better than their best. We must start as a team. We are only as strong as our weakest link. From this point on, let us stand tall together and show the world what we are made of. You show the world what type of people you are. You can act like hoodlums or you can act like men, but remember this, the whole world is watching you." Wanton got up and walked out.

Jamal was the first to speak. "We've got to get it together, fellows. Sarge is right. We have to set an example for others to follow."

Corporal Batts stepped in front of the men. "Okay, fellows, this is what we can do. Let's split up into groups. We will rotate assignments. I want the best marchers with the worst marchers. I want the soldiers that scored the highest on the common task skills with those that scored low— you get my drift."

The band gathered at the old schoolhouse. The drummer sat with his back against the a, sticks in hand, twirling them absently between his fingers. The bass player lay on the grass, looking up at the sky. He'd been practicing earlier, but his guitar still lay on the grass beside him. Pee Wee, reunited with his precious trumpet, spent his time polishing it to a shine.

"I told you Karen was bad news," Will said.

Pee Wee frowned. "Man, you know, that wasn't her fault. You know how soldiers are."

"I suppose," Will replied. He scratched his chin. "What's her deal anyway?"

"What do you mean?"

"On the outside, she's everything that a man wants. I guess you can say that she has a heavenly outer shell, but on the inside, she is full of fire."

Pee Wee chuckled. "She says the same thing about you!"

"What?"

"I guess you could say the two of you are fire and ice," Pee Wee replied.

"I wonder about you sometimes," Will said. "You say some of the craziest things."

"Well, how crazy is this? A man offers your band a recording contract, but you turn it down because you think it will make you lose your freedom."

"Aw, Pee Wee, don't start on that again," Will pleaded.

"Look, I was just making a point," Pee Wee exclaimed.

Bertha and Karen walked up just then. Bertha kissed Pee Wee and sat next to him. Karen, looking nervous, straightened her skirt and had a seat beside Will.

"Well, if it isn't Helen of Troy," Will teased.

"I'm sorry about what happened last night," Karen stated compassionately.

"Sorry? Is that all that you have to say after what you put me through?" Will replied feverishly.

Karen stood up. "What would you have me to do? What's done is done and I can't change that." She quickly exited the area.

"You just ignited that fire," Pee Wee said, smiling.

Will got up to follow her.

Pee Wee played a few notes. "I have a feeling those two are going to be together for a long time."

"But they're not together," Bertha said.

"Not yet," Pee Wee claimed. "Do you know what happens when fire meets ice?"

"Of course," Bertha replied. "The ice melts." Pee Wee nodded his head in agreement.

Will followed Karen until she finally slowed down. Near the capitol building, Karen sat down and put her face into her hands. Will caught up to her and kneeled down beside her. "I'm sorry. I didn't mean to yell at you. I guess you can say that I am still a bit upset about what happened last night. Look, I didn't mean to hurt you, so please don't cry."

A voice screamed out from behind Will, and the words ignited a cold sensation down his spine. "Boy, what have you done to this here young lady?"

Will turned slowly and looked up at a white police officer who stood only a few feet from them. The officer stood firmly over Will, tapping the palm of his left hand with the billy club as if he were ready to use it.

"On your feet, boy," the officer ordered. He poked Will in the side with the billy club. Karen tried to push the club away. "No, don't," she said. Will rose slowly.

"Hands up, boy," the officer ordered. "What are you doing here, boy?" the officer asked as he frisked Will.

A terrified Karen screamed, "We were just talking! We weren't doing anything." She stood up. "Why don't you just leave us alone?"

The officer turned his attention to Karen and poked her in the chest. "Did I ask you anything?" He turned his attention back to Will, narrowing his eyes. "I know you don't have anything on you, but I do know you're up to no good. So I suggest you take this white trash and go home before I throw you in jail."

Karen grabbed Will by the arm and pulled him away. The police officer stood on the steps and watched them scamper away. They walked together for a while in silence, until she stopped beneath a tree. She stood with her back against the tree trunk. Will took a careful step forward so they were face-to-face, only inches from each other. A warm breeze lifted the leaves of the tree and washed her face in a play of shadows and sunshine.

Will drew in a breath. "Look, Karen, I'm sorry about what just happened, but this is the life that we live."

"I understand. I've been a fool for not seeing the obvious unfair treatment our people have been subjected to," Karen replied. "I guess people have seen me as a white person for so long, I have not been subjected to the same treatment as you and others. Yet I could see the signs all around me."

"It's not your fault. Many of our people are victims of a conditioned mind, one that tells us to accept the things as they are and not to stand for the way things should be," Will explained.

"You have really opened up my eyes to some things," Karen admitted.

Will smiled. "Now that your eyes are open, what are you going to do about the things you see?"

Chapter Seven

The next morning at Camp Campbell, everyone on base stood still as the bugle played reveille and the flag was raised. When the bugle stopped playing, everything returned to normal.

Corporal Batts stood in front of the platoon.

"I came up with a motto for our platoon. It came from the talk that SFC Wanton gave to us. The motto is Proud to Be Me. This is what we will be. Proud. We will train hard and work together. So, when you are called to the position of attention, sound off with our new motto. Platoon, attention!"

"Proud to Be Me!" the platoon cried in response.

Corporal Batts ordered the men to march and Jamal to call cadence.

"I'm going to put some stank on it," Jamal promised with a grin.

Upstairs, Hicks stood by his window, listening to the soldiers and watching them move below as they practiced their drill and ceremony with precision. A knock sounded at his door. "Come in."

SFC Wanton walked in. "Sir, you called?"

"Yes, I did," said Hicks. "Come here, have a look." Wanton walked up to the window and looked out.

"Sergeant Wanton, are those your men?" asked Hicks.

"Yes, sir," Wanton replied.

"Sergeant Wanton, you have a group of highly motivated troops. I just had to call you and tell you that I'm impressed."

"Thank you, sir!" Wanton replied.

Moments later, SFC Wanton walked downstairs. Corporal Batts saluted Sergeant Wanton, made an about-face movement, and marched back to the rear of the formation.

"At ease!" Wanton yelled. "Guys, over the past few days you have been doing a great job. However, I feel that you can do much better. The next few days will be very challenging. We will have the range, and we will also be tested on our basic soldier skills. I highly suggest that you carry your common task manuals everywhere that you go and study every chance that you get. Platoon, attention!"

"Proud to Be Me!" the soldiers called in reply.

Wanton, filled with pride, smirked a little and called Corporal Batts.

"Yes, Sergeant!" answered Batts.

"Make sure that the troops are ready for their common task skills test. Keep up the good work, Corporal," Wanton said as he patted Batts on the shoulder and retreated back to the building.

"At ease," the corporal ordered. "For the rest of the day, we are going to practice our common task skills. So, on the command of fall out, I want you to go in and get your common task manuals and be back here so that we can prepare for our common task test. Platoon Attention!"

"Proud to Be Me!" The soldiers ran into the barracks.

The next morning, the post commander called a meeting in General Thomas's office to discuss the looming war and growing protest within the country. A group of white officers (commanding and executive) sat at a table together. The colored noncommissioned officers sat in chairs behind them. The white NCOs stood on the opposite side of the room. The two groups of NCOs ignored each other's presence.

Tension was in the air, as everyone had their own idea of the meeting's agenda, but orders precluded them from speculating.

General Thomas stood and cleared his throat.

"Gentlemen, due to the escalation of the war and the social outcry for equality, the government has decided that a nation divided against itself cannot stand. Therefore, the commander-in-chief has ordered the Pentagon to desegregate the military."

A long moment of stunned silence ensued. The NCOs looked at each other in disbelief. Lieutenant Dukes was the first to speak.

"Sir, if the military is desegregated, will the colored NCOs be demoted?"

General Thomas frowned. "No. The colored NCOs will be treated the same as white NCOs. They will be given the same respect as the white NCOs. Let it be known, if any soldier, white or black, disrespects any NCO, they will be charged with insubordination. And, I will not hesitate to punish anyone who does not adhere to the guidelines set by the Pentagon."

Lt. Dukes looked at his fellow white officers before replying. "Sir, with all due respect, I don't think the American people will allow their sons to be ordered around by *coloreds*. It's just not the natural order of things."

General Thomas regarded Dukes with a stony expression. "The American people do not run this military. Nor are American soldiers in the habit of disregarding orders based on personal opinion or the conventional wisdom of their friends and family. Therefore, there should be no issues and no problems with colored NCOs, nor any soldier in this unit, for that matter. Do I make myself clear?"

Dukes slid back into his seat. The black NCOs glanced at each other in silent amazement.

"Sir," Dukes said, raising his hand, "do you think that these types of changes could affect the morale of the soldiers?"

"No, Lieutenant. I think that these changes will be good for the military as well as the United States. If each soldier does his job as ordered—as we all expect our men to do—there should be no problems at all. It's this simple, Lieutenant, if you can't follow orders handed to you, the military has no use for you," said General Thomas. "An order is an order. Do I make myself clear, Lieutenant?""Sir, how soon will these changes be implemented?" Hicks asked.

"I'm glad you asked, because I was given the task of integrating the first division of the United States Army, effective immediately," said Thomas. "Are there any more questions?" The general took a long look around the room. The colored soldiers looked hopeful, while the white soldiers barely bit back their anger. None were ready to challenge the general or question him further.

"Well, if that's all," the general said. "Sergeant Major."

The sergeant major stood and yelled attention; the soldiers snapped to attention, and the general walked out.

The soldiers walked out of the conference room. Jones, Wanton, and Richards walked down the corridor together. They kept their voices low but were unable to keep silent about what they had just witnessed.

"I can't believe *we* will be given equal command as white non-commissioned officers," Jones said. "It's unheard of. I wonder who made the final decision that this was going to happen, and how hard they had to push."

"We are finally becoming an army united," Wanton replied. "It was bound to happen eventually."

"United, what in the hell do you mean united?" Richards shot back. "You saw the looks on their faces in there when they heard the news?"

Jones nodded in agreement. "You can bet your asses they aren't doing this because they want to. You just heard Dukes in there, didn't you? The white NCOs aren't going to take this well."

As they neared the exit, they stopped in front of the door. This was not a conversation they could have as freely as they would like. Nevertheless, they were elated with the news they had just received.

"Why in the hell do you think they are doing this?" Wanton questioned.

"The pressure from people protesting the Jim Crow laws is finally getting to them," Jones urged. "It has to be. You know, they say that a nation divided against itself cannot stand, and this nation seems to be coming together slowly but surely."

"Man, you all don't know what you are talking about," Wanton declared, exiting the building.

"I hate to say it, but I think Wanton is a little Uncle Tom-ish," Richards said.

"You guys are crazy," Jones replied, chuckling. "Wanton is just playing the game to provide for his family like we all are. Wanton's son is out there on the front line protesting. He had to learn it from his father."

The next day, Will walked downtown with his hands in his pockets, taking in all the old reminders of Jim Crow and his own place as a second-class citizen in the land of the free—the United States, a place his father referred to as the greatest nation in the world. It irritated Will that his father could not see the signs of inequality all around him. No Coloreds Allowed. The signs had been permanent fixtures since he could remember, and they probably wouldn't change if people didn't take action to fight for their rights. Will would be an old man walking with a cane staring at the same signs that haunted his youth if people didn't stand. He knew there was a price for not falling in line, but he was willing to pay it.

Will went to the burger bar and found Pee Wee there with Bertha. They were happily chatting, laughing at some joke Pee Wee had just told. He wished he could feel as happy and carefree as they did. He said hello and sat down beside them.

"Hey, man," Pee Wee said. "Why the sad face?"

"Life. I mean, this world is so cruel," Will replied.

"Oh boy, here we go again," Pee Wee said. "You know, Will, you really have a way of destroying a moment of joy and peace."

"How can you have joy? Take a look around you. Can't you see the inequality? We have to do something," Will snarled.

"What are you going to do, march on Washington?" Bertha asked, laughing, then popped a french fry into her mouth. "Boy, you are a piece of work."

"You know, you sound so much like Dr. Davis, I should call you Lil' Doc, 'cause he was out of his mind, and I think you are losing your mind," Pee Wee said jokingly.

"Wow, you didn't get anything that Dr. Davis taught us, did you?" replied Will.

"Thank God I didn't, because if I did I would be lost like you, my brother, walking around here mad at the world," Pee Wee countered.

Will chuckled. "You know, Dr. Davis once told me that while traveling through my life's journey, there will be rocks and there will be sponges and to never be deterred by the rocks because eventually they will break."

Pee Wee shook his head in disappointment. "Dr. Davis has really messed you up. Wow, what a head job."

"By grasping his knowledge, my eyes were opened, but you are still walking in the dark," Will replied. "Pee Wee, I am not asking you to believe in what I say, I am merely asking you to see things the way they are and stand for the way things should be."

"Will, what do you want me to do? Get my head bashed in for not following the law?" Pee Wee retorted.

"No, I am asking you not to be a victim of terrorism, because it is the fear of those unjust laws that links us to the chains of slavery," explained Will. "And if you continue to accept things the way they are and not stand for righteousness, you will be terrorized for the rest of your life."

"Will, I am sorry, but I am a law-abiding citizen, one that has pledged allegiance to the United States of America, and I in good conscience cannot stand against my own government," rationalized Pee Wee.

"Pee Wee, understand this, I love this country just as much as you do, but there are still things we need to change to make it better. I guarantee you that if we accept things the way they are, things will never change. Don't you remember when Dr. Davis told us there are two kinds of men in this world—those who accept things they cannot change and those who change things they cannot accept? What kind of man are you?"Pee Wee paused for a few moments. "I am the kind of man who is trying to change our situation."

"So, if you are not on the front lines marching and protesting, what are you trying to do to make things better for us?" Will solicited.

"Well, actually, I am trying to get you to understand that money talks." Pee Wee looked Will in the eye "Without money, no one can hear you. So, I suggest that if you want to make a change, sign the contract with the band."

"Aw, come on, Pee Wee, don't start with that today. I don't see how that has anything to do with what we were talking about anyway."

"Just listen for a minute. Everyone has a God-given talent, and ours is music. Through our music, we can start a revolution."

"What are we supposed to do? Sing for equal rights under the law? I don't think so.""Will, you have to understand, the only people that can hear you when you whisper are the people that you are talking to. However, through music you can be heard around the world, sending messages that you want people to hear."

"I . . . I just can't sell myself," replied Will.

"Damn, Will, I wish that you could hear yourself because right now you are not making any sense."

"For the last time, Pee Wee, I am not signing that damn contract." Will looked up and saw people walking toward the stage in the park. "Hey, what's going on?" he asked. "Where are all these people coming from?"

"I don't know. I have never seen so many people here at one time." They moved a little closer to hear the man on stage to find out what was going on. Seeing Karen, they stood next to her. Though she was mostly quiet through the event, Will looked over at her and saw her occasionally nodding her head as she listened attentively to the speeches.

The man who got on the stage was an articulate speaker. He spoke about a young black man being killed by white cops for looking at a white girl. A group of others standing on stage waited to speak after the young man. They were all young, educated people that Will recognized from the community. It was refreshing for Will to see young black men and women talking, taking a stand in society for the justice and fairness of his people.

"Who is he?" Pee Wee asked.

"I don't know," Will replied, "but I bet those brothers and sisters are going to be the matches that starts the fire in our people to stand for our rights."

Will overheard someone in the crowd say the young man was a relative from Chicago of the young man who was shot.

"I'm glad we didn't miss this," Will whispered to Karen. "This is exactly what I've been talking about. Nobody is going to just give us our rights, not without a fight. We must take them, and to do that our people need to stand and be heard. We must demand our rights. Works without deeds is dead."Pee Wee got fidgety when he saw white policemen arrive with riot gear on. "Hey, are you guys ready to go?" he asked.

"No, I want to hear the rest of this," Karen replied. "These people are talking about some important things that are happening in our society."

"Suit yourself, Karen," Bertha replied. "My baby and I are going to get out of this place before something happens, and so should you."

"Don't tell me you are going to let those guys in uniform intimidate you," Will said.

"They can't do anything to us if we don't do anything wrong," Karen added.

"Tell it to the brother they shot," Pee Wee replied as he and Bertha began to walk away.

Karen opened her mouth to speak, but Bertha and Pee Wee had already disappeared into the crowd of people.

"Well, you're stuck with me for a little while, aren't you?" Will smirked.

"I guess I am," she said softly. A little smile tugged at the corners of her mouth.

"I'll walk you home whenever you are ready," Will said.

"I want to stay a little while longer. I really want to hear what these people are talking about."

Will smiled and nodded his head in agreement, noting the subtle change in her. He grabbed her hand and held it.

As sunset came, deepening the skies to a purplish blue hue, loud voices over a bullhorn interrupted the speakers on stage.

"We're asking that you clear this area now," came a voice. "You do not have the right to assemble here. You have five minutes to disperse."

A rolling grumble of discontent sounded from the crowd. "What are you talking about?" people yelled. "We have every right to be here!""What's going on?" Karen asked as they became engulfed in the middle of the chaos swirling around them.

They looked for a way out of the clash between the protestors and the police. Words and debris flew through the crowd as Karen and Will tried to avoid getting hit on their way out of the park. Will saw a police officer a few feet away hit a young man in the head with a billy club. People started throwing glass bottles as officers moved through the crowd, mowing down people with their clubs, pushing down anyone that got in their way. People screamed and cussed.

Will took Karen's hand and they ran.

Once they were a few blocks from the park, Karen stopped, leaning against the outside wall of an apartment building. "Please," she said, "I've got to catch my breath."

Will nodded and stood beside her. The stone wall felt cool against his back. On the street, Will noticed people moving along as normal. Apparently, no one here was privy to what had gone on at the park. After a few minutes, he did see a police car rushing in that direction.

"Come on, let's walk," Will said, grabbing Karen by the hand. "We don't want anyone thinking we're soliciting."

"Yeah, you're right," she said, smoothing one hand over her hair and then over her skirt. Karen looking at Will. "Your shirt is all torn and there's blood all over you! Are you okay? I'm sorry for what you had to endure to get me out of that hostile situation."

"What are you sorry for?" Will asked.

"Look at you." Karen pointed at Will's clothing.

"Yeah," Will replied, gesturing toward himself, "this is not your fault, and it's nothing a couple bandages and a new shirt won't fix. Anyway, I knew they were going to attack these rallies sooner or later."

"How did you know that?" "Anytime two or more of us gather, they feel the need to break us up because there is strength in numbers," Will alleged.

"What are they so afraid of? They have guns and we don't. They even have the law on their side." "They know they couldn't get away with their injustices so easily if we all stood up together," Will replied. "Like Lincoln said, together we stand; divided we fall."

"I don't know about that," Karen said, rubbing her arms as if she felt a chill. "They still outnumber us."

"Yes, but they are united in a campaign to keep those of us who can see and who are not afraid to speak up for equal rights silent."

"Which is exactly why we end up getting gassed and beaten," Karen said bitterly. "Wow, I never realized how devastating our voices could be."

"Why do you think the country is so adamant about keeping us from voting?" Will asked. "The answer is as simple as keeping us silent; in other words, a mute man can't make a sound."

Karen paused for a few moments. "But he can communicate by other means, like having people with louder voices to speak for him, write, or use body language."

"Karen, I enjoy spending time with you, but I really need to get you home, and we need to get off these streets before we are caught by one of those trigger-happy lawmen," Will urged. Karen agreed, and Will continued walking her to Bertha's home.

"If my dad knew about what happened today, he would kill me," Karen said.

"Are you going to tell him?" Will asked.

"Of course not!"

"Then how will they know?"Karen cracked a smile. "I guess they won't because I know Bertha will not tell."

By the dawning of the day, they arrived at Bertha's house. In an effort to conceal her soiled and tattered clothing, Karen walked to the side of the house with Will. Karen put her hands on the windowsill and turned toward Will. "Are you going to give me a boost?" she asked.

"Is that all you want?" Will asked, cupping his hand to let her step into and through the window. "I could come in and comfort you if you like," he proposed."That won't be necessary. I need a little time to wind down from the events of the day. I am still a little shaken."

They'd both had a long day, and their nerves had been frayed by the events they'd experienced.

Bertha sat up in her bed when she saw Karen's tattered and soiled clothes. "What happened to you? Did Will try and take advantage of you? I knew he was a pervert! Just wait until I see him. I am going to give him a piece of my mind!"

Karen called out, "Bertha! It wasn't his fault. We were just sitting listening to the people speak when, all of a sudden, police came in riot gear and threw tear gas and forced people out of the park."

"Wow! Why on earth did the police do that? They had to have a reason.""They were telling us we didn't have a permit to assemble and we had to leave, so some people started talking back and resisting. That is when the confrontation started," Karen exclaimed. "Will got hit with a bottle someone threw. We were fortunate enough to get out of there almost unscathed.""Wow! I am glad Pee Wee and I left when we did," Bertha said. "Why did you stay anyway?"

Karen searched deep for an excuse. "I don't know . . . I guess you could just say that I . . . I was curious about the reason so many of our people were standing in solidarity."

"You know what I think? I think you wanted to stay because of Will," Bertha replied. "He got to you, didn't he?"

"What? Girl. No," Karen said. She sat down on the bed and took off her shoes. Then she stripped down to her slip. Bertha sat on the opposite twin-sized bed, facing her.

"Mm hmm." Bertha nodded. "You know, you have been changing since you met him; as a matter of fact, you are starting to act like him."

"Girl, please. Will has done nothing to me. My eyes are being opened to the ills of our society."

"You can say whatever you want, but I know your ill of society begins with a W and he has you," Bertha replied. Her nerves had been frayed by the day's events as well.

Gloria enjoyed sitting out on the front porch after twilight, getting a breath of fresh air and watching the clouds drift past the moon on this quiet evening. Swaying in her rocking chair, she hummed church hymns as she knitted. She felt at peace, relieved that the chores of the day were done.

Gloria heard her husband's feet pound the ground. She could recognize his steps anywhere. Sure enough, she soon saw his figure emerge from beneath the shadows of the trees that lined their street. Bill walked up the steps and laid a kiss on her cheek.

"Why are you home so early?" she asked.

"I couldn't wait to tell you the good news," he said, taking a seat on the stoop. "Honey, you are looking at a man that has the same authority as white NCOs. We are finally being treated as equals in the military."

Gloria was about to congratulate him when she saw their son walking up the street. She stood and tapped her husband's shoulder. "Will!" she cried, running down the sidewalk to meet him. He was bloody, his shirt torn, and his eyes were wild with shock and adrenaline. Bill didn't move from his spot on the stoop.

"Boy, what in the hell happened to you?" Wanton demanded.

"I don't know, Pop. We were all hanging out at the park, and all of a sudden a bunch of police came and said that we couldn't assemble there. We told them that we could assemble anywhere we pleased. Then they shot tear gas, hit people with clubs, and arrested some, too."

"See boy, I done told you 'bout hanging out with those protestors. See what you get?"

"Bill!" Gloria cried, exasperated. "Come on, son, let's get you inside. Let me look at these wounds."

"I'll be all right, Mom." Will sighed. "Pop, we were not protesting; we were just standing for our rights. We love this country as much as anyone does, but we want to be treated fairly. We want our nation to live up to the promises it made."

"Really? You've got a funny way of showing it. Tell me something. If you love this country so damn much, why do you keep embarrassing me singing about how unfair the country is and hanging out with those troublemakers?" "If we got fair treatment in this country; then we couldn't sing about unfair treatment, nor would we have a reason to protest," Will replied.

"All right, you keep on going down to that damn park protesting if you want to. I'm telling you right now, if they throw your ass in jail, I'm not going down there to get you out again," Wanton bellowed.

"Sometimes we must make sacrifices to change things that we cannot accept," Will said. "Moses made a sacrifice when he denounced his royal status and embraced his heritage to free the children of Israel. The least that I can do is sacrifice a little of my time for a worthy cause such as equal treatment for all people."

"Well you are not Moses, and there is no need for you to sacrifice anything. All you have to do is be patient, because all things will change in time."

"Pop, Professor Davis told me a long time ago that work without deed is dead." Wanton shook his head in disappointment. "Doctor Davis really done a job on your head."

Gloria tried to steer her son into the house, but he got free of her grip and went back to where his father stood. "Pop, you must understand. Time doesn't make changes; people make changes. If you spend your time waiting on it, time will pass you by, and you just get old watching all your dreams die."

"Son, what is your life if you spend it in and out of jail?" asked Gloria.

Wanton took off his hat and scratched his head. He sat back down, and Will sat beside him.

"Pop, my life is life is not worth living if I don't stand for those things that I believe in."

"Are your beliefs worth losing your freedom?" asked Wanton"How can I lose my freedom if I never had it to begin with? Freedom is an illusion in our society; separate but equal does not equal freedom."

Will got up and walked into the house. Wanton looked up at his wife. "What happened, Gloria? Where'd I go wrong with him?"His wife smiled softly at him. She sat down beside him and squeezed his hand. "You did nothing wrong. You will just have to learn to trust that our son will make the right decisions. He's not the only young person who thinks the way he does.""I just want him to make something out of his life. I don't want him to be some bum out on a corner playing music for change. I want him to do great things," explained Wanton.

"He will, I'm sure of it."

The barracks were busy as some soldiers packed their bags. No one had an explanation as to why they were packing or where they were going, and while some were anxious about what was happening, all gathered their things as quickly as possible. All kinds of rumors were going around: they were being sent away for a training exercise or being sent to a new base. Speculation only added to the men's anxiety.

"Hey, Corporal, what's going on?" Jamal asked.

"I don't know."

"Are they being sent to some kind of special unit?" Platt asked.

"All I know is that SFC Wanton wants me to march these guys down to division headquarters."

The soldiers hugged one another as they all left the barracks with their gear and their duffel bags on their backs. Corporal Batts marched the soldiers down the street.

"Keep your head up!" Pvt. Jamal yelled.

When Corporal Batts arrived at the division's headquarters, Captain Hicks, SFC Wanton, and LT Dukes walked out of the office.

"Corporal Batts," Wanton said, "file the men in here."

Batts ordered the men to march into the building. A group of white soldiers filed out of the building and fell into formation behind Batts. Confused, Batts turned. "Hey, you're in the wrong formation. Did you hear me? You're in the wrong formation."

"Fall in, Corporal," Wanton ordered.

"But Sarge . . ."

"Fall in!" he commanded. Batts went to the end of the formation while Wanton took over.

"Right face! Forward march!"

As they marched down the street, Batts gave cadence, but the white soldiers remained silent, refusing to respond.

Pvt. Jamal saw the white soldiers marching down the street under Wanton's command. "What the . . . ?"

The other soldiers turned and looked as well.

Wanton suppressed a small grin. "Platoon halt. Right face. At ease. Corporal Batts, get the rest of the soldiers out here."

Batts ran into the barracks to get the remaining soldiers. They ran out and fell into formation just as the other soldiers did.

Wanton called out, "Everybody gather around. Bring it in. This is the new face of the United States Army, and hopefully it will one day be the face of America. A man once said, 'A nation divided against itself cannot stand.' In this platoon there will be only one color, and that color is green. I will accept nothing but the best from you both individually and collectively. With that being said, I want the soldiers that already live here to help the new soldiers set up their living spaces and make them feel at home. Tomorrow I will expect all of you to be ready at 0500. Platoon, attention! Fall out!"

The soldiers went into the barracks together. As soon as they were inside, a white soldier threw his bag on Pvt. Jamal's bunk.

"You see that this bunk already belongs to someone. So why in the fuck did you throw your gear on it?" asked Pvt. Jamal.

The white private, a man named Hamilton, shrugged and grinned at Jamal. "Because it's the bunk I want."

"Well look here, you're not home where you can have it your way. So I see it like this," Jamal said, stepping close enough that they were face-to-face. "You can move your shit now or you can take an ass whipping and move your shit later."

Hamilton stared at Jamal for a long moment. Losing their battle of wills, Hamilton grabbed his bag and walked away.

Jamal nodded at Platt. "What's wrong with this motherfucker, coming in here thinking that he is going to take over?"

Johnson helped a white soldier, Taylor, to arrange his things in one of the lockers. Smith threw his bag down on the floor and put a foot up on the bottom of one of the bunks. "Hey boy, when you finish helping him, you can get started on mine."

Johnson ignored Smith. Taylor looked from Johnson to Smith. He remained silent but shifted uncomfortably on his feet.

"You hear me talking to you, *boy*," Smith snarled. All of the black soldiers looked at Smith.

"I'm not a boy. I'm a man," Johnson replied.

The black soldiers surrounded Pvt. Smith's bunk. He rose to his feet, defiant, chest puffed out. "Do you boys know who I am?"

"We don't care," Jamal assured him. "Did you hear anybody fucking ask you?"

"Well, I am John Smith Jr., the oldest son of John Smith. My father owns one of the largest plantations in Missi—"

"You must be out of your damned mind," Jamal cut him off. "This isn't your plantation, and we aren't your boys. So I highly suggest that you get off your ass and do your own work. Nobody is impressed."

"Man. Just stupid." Johnson sighed. "Maybe he's looking for a reason to get beat up."

Wanton and Dukes walked into the barracks just then.

"Attention!" Wanton called.

Smith looked over at Dukes and then smiled at Jamal, as if he were about to get away with something.

Will and Pee Wee sat together in the park, Karen and Bertha joined them.

When Pee Wee saw Karen's face, he exclaimed, "Aw hell, naw. Will got to you, too!"

Karen sat down beside Will. He looked at her, tipped her chin with his fingertip, and saw "black" written on the left side of her cheek and "proud" written on the right. Will smiled and pointed. "What is this?"

"It is my first step into taking a stand for the fair treatment of our people," Karen answered.

Pee Wee whispering to Bertha, "Your cousin has lost her damn mind."

"Does it bother you, Pee Wee? Are you ashamed of who you are?" Karen asked.

"No, I'm proud of who I am," Pee Wee replied.

"Then why do the words on my face annoy you?" Karen asked.

"It doesn't annoy me. You just look like a damn fool with that written on your face." "Pee Wee, I wish you could hear some of the words that come out of your mouth sometimes; the words written on Karen's face are no different from the color of our skin that people see every day," Will interjected.

Pee Wee frowned. "Will, you know that wasn't what I meant."

"No, I don't. Why don't you enlighten me?"

"Why in the hell would we write our skin color on our skin when people can simply look at us and automatically know that we are black?" "Can you look at Karen and tell she is black? Believe it or not, we come in all shades of color." "What?" Pee Wee said, irritated.

"Ah, why are you picking on my baby?" Bertha said, hugging Pee Wee.

"You know what, Bertha? Let's go, baby."

Will and Karen both shook their heads as the couple walked off.

"They'll see," Karen told Will once their friends were out of earshot.

"Yes, maybe one day," he replied. "I hope they do. So, what inspired you to wear your pride on your face?"

"Well, my skin is light, and people sometimes question my race. I wrote this on my face to let everyone know that I am not ashamed of any part of my heritage," explained Karen.

"It's funny you said that. Most blacks are born with dark skin. Although blacks have done great things throughout history, some are still in denial as to who they are." He put an arm around her shoulders.

"This world is so crazy," Karen said, barely above a whisper.

"Sometimes," Will sighed, "I don't think it's worth living. Not if we have to look at it from under someone else's boot."

"Don't say that," Karen pleaded, "because you and only you can control your destiny. Things are hard, but you still have choices to make."

"I know," he said. "But we are at a great disadvantage by being black in America," Will added.

"All that means is that we have to work harder to achieve our goals. Most of us are using the uneven playing field as an excuse for our failures."

Lt. Dukes walked into the barracks. The soldiers were silent, waiting to hear what he was about to say.

"At ease. Men, I just came to see how well you are all adapting to your new quarters."

"Sir, Pvt. Smith requests permission to speak."

"Speak, soldier," commanded Dukes.

"Sir, is this some form of punishment? I mean, is there a reason that we must stay in the same barracks with these animals?"

"Who in the fuck are you calling an animal?" Jamal cried. He moved forward, fists curled, chest out. Wanton moved in front of Jamal, blocking him from getting near Smith.

"At ease, soldier," Dukes ordered. "Sergeant Wanton, you need to get control of your men."

Dukes turned back to Smith. "Son, I know that this is difficult, but the Pentagon insists that we must become an army of one in order to be one of the greatest fighting forces ever. We have our commands, and if we want to be good soldiers, we have to abide by them."

"So we must set our differences aside and work together," Wanton interjected.

Wanton and Dukes left the barracks. The moment they were gone, Jamal warned Smith, "This shit ain't over."

Outside the barracks, Wanton and Dukes were having a confrontation of their own. Dukes lit a cigarette and purposely blew the smoke in Wanton's face. He noticed that one of Dukes's hands was shaking.

"Sergeant Wanton! Do you have a problem with whites?" Dukes asked.

"No, sir," replied Wanton.

"Then I expect you to treat those white soldiers how white soldiers should be treated," exclaimed Dukes. "Sir, in my eyes there are no white or black soldiers; they are all American soldiers. I will treat them all the same," Wanton retorted.

"Yes, you better, 'cause I got my eyes on you," Dukes proclaimed. He flicked his cigarette butt on the ground, crushed it beneath his boot, turned, and walked away.

Wanton sighed with relief and walked back into the barracks to order the men to assemble in formation outside.

The soldiers all screamed and ran for the door. They fell into formation. SFC Wanton walked outside to find two squads of white soldiers and two squads of black soldiers.

"On the command of fall out, I want you to break up into two groups. I want one group to my left and one group to my right. Fall out!"

All the white soldiers ran to the left of SFC Wanton, and all the black soldiers ran to the right.

Wanton, hands behind his back, stepped forward to address the soldiers. "This is the face of a young, ignorant nation—a nation that believes that one group is superior to the other group, but too naive to know that all men are created equal. So let me end this by saying that I am no better than any of you, and none of you are any better than me. To prove my point, fall back into formation."

Wanton ordered the black and white soldiers to face one another within formation.

"Open ranks, march!" Wanton yelled. "From now on, the people that you are facing will be your battle buddies. You will be bunk mates. You will know your buddies better than you know yourselves. One day you will find that you are more similar than you think. Corporal—"

Wanton turned as a runner came up to address him.

"Sergeant Wanton! Sergeant Wanton! LT Dukes and Captain Hicks need to see you ASAP."

"Corporal Batts, ensure that these soldiers remain paired. I want a list of each pair."

The runner escorted Wanton to Captain Hicks's office. He knocked on the door and requested permission to come in.

"Enter!" Hicks called out.

SFC Wanton opened the door and closed it behind him. He stood two feet in front of Captain Hicks's desk and rendered a hand salute.

"Sir, Sergeant Wanton reporting."

"Take a seat, Sergeant," Hicks replied.

Wanton already felt the tension in the room. He would like to have known what Dukes and Hicks were talking about prior to his arrival, but he had the unpleasant feeling he'd find out soon enough. He took the only empty seat in front of the desk, next to Lt. Dukes.

"Gentlemen, I just received orders from the Pentagon that we have seventy-two hours to deploy to Korea."

Wanton leaped out of his chair. "Sir, our troops are not ready! To send our troops now would be suicide. My men weren't able to get shooting practice in the last—"

"Sergeant Wanton! The enemy isn't going to wait for you to get ready to fight. *You* should always be prepared," Dukes hissed.

Captain Hicks ignored Dukes and leaned forward, hands clasped, his look one of sincere apology. "Sergeant Wanton, I understand your concerns. However, my hands are tied. But I also have faith in you."

"Don't worry about a thing, sir," Dukes said. "I will lead the men to a swift and decisive victory."

Both Wanton and Hicks looked at Dukes, befuddled.

Will and Karen rode a bus through an urban housing area. Some drunks hung out in front of the local bar passing around brown bags of liquor. Some people in the alley threw dice and smoked pot, while others sat on the stoops of their houses just watching time pass them by. Different religious sects tried to spread the gospel. Will was depressed by the sight of these people, but he didn't comment. Some people had made their homes in this place, and he didn't feel comfortable judging them without knowing their stories.

His mother's words came back to him, about his father working hard to provide a good home for their family. He hadn't ever stopped to wonder what kind of work his father would have done if he weren't in the army. Jobs were limited for a colored man, more so back when his father was Will's age. How easy was it to end up in a neighborhood like this one if you didn't have a job or you had one that didn't pay much? Will squeezed Karen's hand and made a silent promise to himself that this would never be the stopping point in his own life.

A preacher stood on the corner handing out pamphlets to people passing by him as he cried out at the top of his lungs, "I know that times are hard, but people, I have a message for you today. If you find yourself lost with no place to go, try GOD. If you're lonely with no one to talk to, try GOD. If you're sick and tired of people trampling all over you, try GOD. There are only two ways that we can do things in this life. There is a right way and there is a wrong way. The right answer to all our problems can only be found in GOD. I know that some of you may be asking, 'Where is this God? Why is he letting us suffer so?' Sometimes God allows us to struggle," the preacher continued.

"Seems like every city has a neighborhood like this," Karen said. "Or worse, a few neighborhoods like it."

"I guess they do," Will said sadly. "You ever think that will change?"

Karen frowned. "I don't know. You just have to wonder why there's so many poor people in a rich country like ours. Is it that people are not trying or is the system broken?"

"I would venture to say that the system is broken, designed to keep the poor struggling and the money in the hands of the rich," Will asserted.

Karen blinked. "I guess I'm just beginning to see things are more complicated than they look."

Now evening, Gloria lay on her couch reading her Bible. Feeling sleepy, she pinched the skin between her eyebrows, trying to bring her vision to sharper focus on the Good Book. She read the gospel of John and came across 3:16: For God so loved the world . . .

Her husband walked into the house, head down, dragging his feet. She sat up, and he kissed her cheek.

"You okay, honey?" she asked, her voice barely above a whisper. He took his time before answering, taking off his jacket and untying his boots.

"I'm tired," Wanton said. "I just want to sit here for a minute and rest."

"Rough day?" she asked.

SFC Wanton nodded his head and laid it upon Gloria's bosom. He looked up at his wife. "Have I told you how much I love you lately?"

"What? The last time I heard those words come from your mouth was twenty years ago when we got married." Gloria relaxed. She lazily rubbed his head as he leaned against her chest. It wasn't often that he let her just baby him. "And by the way, it wouldn't kill you to say it more often," she teased. "A woman occasionally likes to be reminded of these things."

Will walked in, passing the living room doorway. He took a double take, walked back, and looked at his parents.

"Ugh. Why don't you go to the room? Nobody wants to see you two drooling all over one another."

"Will, come in here for a minute," Wanton called. He sat up and gazed at his son.

Will walked back in and carefully took a seat on the edge of his father's chair so that he faced both parents on the sofa. He crossed his arms, planting his feet against the floor.

"Son, I know that I've been hard on you," Wanton said. "I just want to take this opportunity to tell you that I love you."

Puzzled, Will dropped into the chair. He looked over at his mother, who seemed as confused by this development as he was. "Dad, are you feeling all right?" Will asked. "I've never felt better," replied Wanton. "I just want you guys to know that I love you very much."

"That's it. What's wrong?" Gloria asked. "What is it you're not telling us?"

"Are you dying of something?" Will asked.

Wanton stood up. "Aw, come on, guys, give me a break. Can I just show you how much I love you?"

Gloria and Will shared a glance of curiosity.

"Well, Dad, if there's nothing wrong, then I have to go." Will got up to leave.

"Wait," Wanton said, motioning his son to sit back down. "Just hold on a minute, I have something to tell you." He stood and began to pace in a small circle. Gloria gave her son a sidelong glance. Moments passed as Wanton tried to figure out how to break the news.

"We're still waiting," Will urged.

"Okay, as you know, Korea is at war," Wanton began.

"What does that have to do with us?" Will asked.

"For one thing, their freedom is at stake," said Wanton.

"What about our people here?" Will countered. "We have our own problems here with the Jim Crow laws and inequality."

"Will . . . just listen! Our government wants to stop the spread of communism."

"What does that have to do with us?" Will asked. "That country should deal with their own problems, just as we should deal with ours."

"We have to defend the interest of the United States by trying to preserve freedom for those who want to be free," asserted Wanton.

Will and Gloria exchanged a look of shock.

"How can you go off and defend the freedom of some other country when you aren't free in your own?" Will leapt from his seat. "Are you going to honestly tell me that makes sense to you?"

"Son, I took an oath to fight for this great nation," Wanton tried to explain.

"This nation? What has this nation done for you, or any of us for that matter?" Will declared

"This nation has allowed me to do a job so I could put a roof over your head and food in your mouth."

Will shook his head in disbelief. "You really don't get it, do you? They're using you, and you just let them." He turned and ran for the door.

"Boy, don't you walk away from me when I am talking to you!" Wanton started to follow his son, but Gloria grabbed his arm.

"Don't do that. Let him be. You just put a lot on his mind; he'll come around," Gloria declared. Wanton sighed and sat back down on the couch. "When are you leaving?" Gloria asked.

"Within the next three days."

"What?" she cried. Gloria paused, trying to compose herself. She continued in a cooler tone. "I know you are just trying to provide for your family."

"I wish someone would explain that to your son," Wanton said, rubbing his chin.

"He is your son, too! I mean, he's just like you; can't you see that's where he gets his stubbornness from?" Gloria stated.

"Don't get me started on him," begged Wanton.

"He just sees things differently," Gloria said, rubbing his back. He leaned against her, still upset but calmed by his wife's touch.

"That boy doesn't know shit," Wanton muttered. "I've been trying to teach him what the world's about, but he's got these preconceived notions in that hard head of his. Tell me, what is a man to do? If I fight for the country that I love in order to support my family, I'm wrong. On the other hand, my son thinks I am a sellout if I fight for the freedom of another country when we don't have equal treatment here."

Pee Wee and Bertha were sharing a quiet moment at his place. On the couch together, he laid his head in Bertha's lap, and she absently ran her hand over his hair when Will burst through the door.

Pee Wee jumped up. "What in the hell is going on?"

"My father! Can you believe he is going to fight for the freedom of another country when we are not free here?"

"Hold on, Will. Slow down and explain to us what is going on," Pee Wee implored.

"My dad and his unit are going to be shipped off to another country to fight their war," Will explained.

Bertha leaped to her feet. "What?"

Pee Wee scratched his head. "Damn, Will, I am sorry to hear that. I wish there were something I could do."

"How could a man take an oath to defend a country founded on hypocrisy?" Will said as he sat down.

"Maybe to put a roof over your head and food in your stomach," Pee Wee said. "Everybody's got to find a way to pay their bills, and I hate to be the one to remind you, but that is his job."

"Ever think about that?" Bertha added. She lowered her voice to a whisper and spoke to Pee Wee. "Anyway, does he ever think about knocking?"

Will clenched his jaw. The truth was, he had thought about the sacrifices his father had made for him and his mother, but he hadn't come up with an answer that satisfied him. Countless times he wondered what had possessed his father to join the army. He couldn't believe there wasn't another job he could have taken. Will always thought his father could have chosen another path to success.

"I don't know, Pee Wee. Maybe my father can run away or something," Will suggested.

"Man, they will put your father in jail faster than you could blink an eye; remember your man Dr. Davis," Pee Wee verbalized.

"The bottom line, your father needs you, now more than ever," Bertha said. "I'm sure he's not happy about having to go either."

"You are both right. I guess I better go and apologize." Will got up and headed for the door.

"That's right, you better apologize before you get that ass whipped," Pee Wee said, settling back down on Bertha's lap.

"By who? I'm a grown man. Those ass-whipping days are over."

Will left and closed the door behind him. Pee Wee grinned at Bertha. "His dad is going to whip that ass when he gets home."

When Will arrived home, the front door was open and his parents still sat on the couch. Only one light was on in the living room, casting a warm glow. His parents both looked up when he came inside. There was an uneasy moment when the three of them looked at each other without speaking.

"Dad, I know why you do what you do, and I appreciate everything that you have done for us," Will asserted. "But I think there has to be a better way to support your family."

"Well, tell me!" Wanton cried. "What would you have me do?" Gloria grabbed his arm, attempting to calm him down. He didn't get up, but his eyes flashed with anger.

"There are other jobs," Will said quietly.

"But this is the job that I chose. I don't want to fight, but I will if my country asks me to defend its interests. I will do it with pride."

Will went to his room, picked up his guitar, and sat down to play. He had nothing else to say. He could hear his parents talking to each other in hushed tones. No doubt his father was still mad at him, but he hadn't done anything but speak the truth. As he strummed his guitar, he closed his eyes and felt the melody, felt the tension in his shoulders and back begin to ease. He doubted his father realized how he hated fighting with him, but he refused to back down from his beliefs. His convictions were the only thing he could really call his own that couldn't be taken away.

Will heard a knock at his window. He got up, pulled back the curtain, and opened the window. "Pee Wee?" Shocked to see him, he said, "What are you doing here?"

"I have a brilliant idea, and it's too good to wait to tell you. I found a way to keep your father out of this war."

"Oh yeah, how is that?" asked Will, a little excited.

"Before I go on, you have to promise to hear me out," Pee Wee requested.

Curious, Will put aside his guitar. "Okay, I'm all ears."

"You know, after you left my house, I did some thinking. Do you remember this?" Pee Wee took a piece of paper from his pocket and waved it at Will.

"Come on, Pee Wee, I thought we already discussed this. I am not going to sell my soul to the devil."

"Think about this. How do you think those little rich kids avoid going to war?" Pee Wee asked.

"I don't know," replied Will.

"You know damn well why those kids don't go to war," Pee Wee declared.

"Because they are white," Will stated.

"You are absolutely right," replied Pee Wee.

"Pee Wee, my dad is black. How is color going to help him?" Will asked.

Pee Wee grinned. "It is true your father doesn't have the right color on his skin to get out of this war, but he can get it," Pee Wee alleged.

"Pee Wee, what's my father to do, put powder on his face to try and pass for being white?" Will asked.

"No, you fool, the color of your skin is not what can get your father out of this situation; it's the color the world appreciates," Pee Wee declared.

"And what color is that, Pee Wee?"

"The color of money . . . green!" Pee Wee said, giggling, "It's the color the world loves."

"So, you are saying I need to be rich in order to keep my father from going to war . . . and how are we supposed to do that?" Will asked.

Pee Wee held up the paper again and shook it. Will sighed and sat down on his bed. Pee Wee climbed in through the window.

"I mean, come on, man, at least think about it. I know how you feel about signing a contract, but think about what it would do for your dad. This could change everything."

Will nodded. "You have a very good point. I'll seriously think about it."

"All right," Pee Wee said. "Do that. I know you'll come to the right decision."

Will watched as Pee Wee crawled back out the window and disappeared down the road. Sighing heavily, he closed the window, pulled the curtains shut, and fell back into his bed.

Chapter Eight

"I am so relieved Will has come to his senses," Wanton said.

It was morning, Wanton and Gloria sat at the kitchen table, Wanton with his coffee and a newspaper, while Gloria removed the last few strips of bacon from the sizzling skillet.

"I told you the Lord always works things out," Gloria said as she looked over her shoulder. She pulled a plate down from the cabinet and fixed a plate. Eggs, bacon, grits, toast, hash browns. Wanton smiled as she placed the meal in front of him.

"God is good, and so is the wonderful woman who cooked this delicious breakfast." He smiled.

"Good morning, everybody," Will said as he walked into the kitchen.

"How is my boy today?" Wanton asked.

"Good, Pop," Will replied, patting his father's shoulder. He walked over to his mother and gave her a kiss on the cheek. "What do you have here? It smells good." He grabbed a plate and piled on a generous helping. He squinted at the bright morning light flooding in through the window. "Wow. It's a beautiful day."

"Yes, Lord, I have to thank Jesus, for every day is beautiful," Gloria replied.

Will took a seat beside his father. "I would like to thank Jesus for giving me the best parents in the world."

"Lord, I don't know what you are doing," Wanton said as he looked to the sky, "but whatever you are doing, keep on doing it."

"Mom, this is delicious as usual," Will uttered.

"Thanks, baby," Gloria replied with a puzzled look on her face.

Wanton took a look at the clock. "I hate to rush, but I'm going to have to go. We have an important meeting today." He kissed his wife on the cheek and left. Gloria walked to the kitchen window and watched him walk away. Sighing, she turned on the faucet and started to wash dishes.

Will shook his head. "There he goes. The man on a mission preparing to go off and fight for our freedom in a foreign land while here we sit oppressed in our own."

"Don't start that again; give your father a break," Gloria said. "Right now, he doesn't need your criticism; he needs your support."

"Mom, what if Dad didn't have to go off to war?" Will stated.

Gloria turned to him. "That would be great, but what can you do to keep him from going to war."

"You'll see in due time," explained Will.

"Son, you know your father is the type of man who has to fight his own battles," declared Gloria.

"Everyone needs a helping hand from time to time," replied Will, "and I may have the power to help Dad."

Gloria reached for a dish towel to dry her hands. "What exactly are you talking about? How are you supposed to help your dad get out of going to war? You know he doesn't have a choice in the matter."

"Everybody has choices. If rich kids don't have to go to war, neither does he," Will replied with confidence.

Gloria came back to the table and sat down. "Honey. Those are rich people. Look around us. We don't have that kind of money."

"Well, I know somebody who knows somebody who knows . . . somebody who has the authority to keep Dad out of this."

"Well, if you can keep your father from going to war, I will be grateful for the rest of my life," Gloria replied.

"Mom, you just leave it to me. I'm going to work miracles like Jesus." Will stood and kissed her cheek. "That was delicious as usual. I wish I could stay and chat longer, but I have miracles to perform."

Will left, and Gloria just shook her head and smiled with a puzzled look on her face. "If that boy isn't just like his daddy," she said to herself.

Gloria got up, cleared the rest of the dishes from breakfast, and had just finished cleaning up when her husband came back in. Her heart dropped. From the serious expression on his face and the swiftness of his movements, she knew something was wrong. He rushed past her and into the bedroom. She followed on his heels.

"It's today. I have to get my things," Wanton said.

"Wha . . . what?" Gloria stuttered. "You mean they're sending you away now? Why so soon?"

"We got the call today," Wanton replied. He reached into the closet and yanked his uniforms off their hangers, shoving them haphazardly into a duffel bag. Pausing, he turned to his wife and pulled her into his arms. "I don't know, but one thing I'm sure about. I love you very much." He kissed her. Gloria hugged him and began to cry. She held onto him tight, catching the scent of his soap and aftershave, trying to hold on to the feeling of being in his arms. She thanked God for her husband and hated to let him go, not knowing when and if he would ever return. She had hoped he would serve his career in the military without leaving her side.

Wanton held tightly to his wife, "Why are you crying?" he asked, not knowing if he would ever return. "You know I am only going for a little while. You know there is no ocean wide enough to keep me from getting back to you." She smiled and hugged him tighter.

"What about Will?" she asked, wiping at her tears with the back of her hand.

"Tell him I love him and to take good care of you while I'm gone," Wanton said in a somber voice.

"Who's going to take care of you?" Gloria asked. Her voice broke. She didn't want to show him how upset she was, but at the moment she couldn't help it.

He smiled and pointed to the sky, and then gave her one last kiss before grabbing his bag and walking out the door.

Gloria stood on the porch and watched her husband disappear down the street knowing she might never see him again. Burdened with the thought of losing her husband forever, she went into the kitchen, sat down at the table, and cried.

Gloria was shaken by the sound of footsteps on her back porch. In an anxious panic, she hoped that her husband had returned. Will ran through the kitchen door, letting it slam behind him. "I got it!" he said. "Mom! I got it!"

Gloria lifted her head to Will with tears streaming down her face. Will knelt beside her and put one of his hands on her back. "Mom, what's wrong?"

Gloria wiped some of the flowing tears from her face, "Your dad. He's gone."

"What?" Will yelled in terror. "What do you mean he's gone?"

Gloria, still crying, said, "His company received the orders to deploy today, so he came home, packed his clothes, said he loved us, and left."

"What?" Will bellowed. "I have to catch him. When did he leave?"

"A couple hours ago," Gloria replied. "Will, what is going on?"

"Mom, I have the papers," Will waved the papers in the air, "signed by the commanding general that excuses Pop from this deployment."

"You what?" Gloria screamed with excitement. "How? I don't understand."

"We met the owner of a record company who knows the commanding general who said that he would get pop out of this deployment if I signed a contract with his record company, so I signed the contract to keep Dad from going on this deployment," Will explained.

Gloria looked at him with hope shining in her eyes. "Well go! Maybe you can catch him before he leaves." Gloria stood and yelled, "Thank you, Jesus!" as Will ran out of the house in search of his father.

Will ran as if his own life depended on it. He reached Pee Wee's home, jumped onto the porch, and ran through the door without knocking. Pee Wee was in the living room with Bertha and Karen, practicing dance moves. They looked up at him, startled. Will bent over for a moment, clutching his knees in an attempt to catch his breath. "Pee

Wee," he said, panting, "I have to get to the base ASAP! I need your help." He held up the contract.

"Is that what I think it is?" Pee Wee asked. His eyes grew wide.

"Yes," Will said.

"My man! That's what I'm talking about!" Pee Wee grabbed Bertha around the waist and twirled her around. He punctuated the move by a couple of high notes from his horn. "We're in the money," Bertha said, clapping her hands and dancing.

"Pee Wee! I need your help. I have to get to the base."

Karen frowned. "What's wrong?"

"I've got to get to the base," Will explained. "I have a waiver that excused my dad from going on this deployment, but my mom says he's going to leave tonight."

"The bus just left!" Karen stated. "There's not another one for an hour."

Pee Wee snapped his fingers. "I know! We'll get Mr. Peavy to take us. Come on."

"Well, let's go!" Will screeched.

Tears slowly dripped from the sky as Will, Pee Wee, Karen, and Bertha ran to Club 6661 to see if they could find Mr. Peavy.

The club wasn't open, but luckily, Peavy was inside cleaning up. Will rushed through the door, trying to explain to Mr. Peavy that he needed his help to get him to base.

"Son, you're babbling. You're talking so fast, I only got half of what you're saying," Peavy said, patting Will's shoulder.

"Bottom line is we've got to get to the base right now," Will explained. "My father's unit is being deployed right now!"

"All right, I'll take you," Peavy said. "Let me lock up and we'll be on our way."

By the time they reached the base, the rain was pouring. A large formation of soldiers marched in unison. Will got out of the car and ran behind the soldiers, screaming for his father.

A guard at the gate stopped him.

"You can't go there!" the soldier screamed. "You're not allowed here; only army personnel."

"You don't understand! My dad! I've got to see him!" Will explained.

"No, you're not listening. You're not allowed onto the base," replied the soldier.

The soldier called for help, and a second soldier came up to help him detain Will. He kept screaming, and his father heard him.

Wanton came running back to the gate. "Men, you can release him. He's my son. He doesn't mean any harm."

"Dad," Will said, "I'm so glad I caught you." He held up the papers and bent at the waist. "You don't have to go."

"What are you talking about?" asked Wanton.

"I signed a recording contract with the owner of a record company who knows your commanding general; he said that he would get your commander to sign a waiver to keep you from deploying. I signed the contract, and here it is," Will said, holding up the waiver. "So you don't have to go."

"Son," Wanton said, putting his hands on his son's shoulders, "I appreciate what you have done, but I must go because it is my duty as an American soldier. The greatest sacrifice a man can make for his country is to give his life for it."

"But what about your family?" Will asked as tears flowed from his eyes like the rains falling from the sky.

"The things that I do are because I love you," Wanton said as he faded off into the pool of soldiers marching off to war.

Will stood speechless and puzzled with his wet paper in hand as the rain continued to shower him.

Karen walked over with an umbrella and put her arm around him. They stood watching the soldiers as they bordered the C-130 airplanes with their weapons for what felt like a long time.

"You okay?" she asked as she tried to wake him from his childhood nightmare that had haunted him for so long. Disappointed, Will nodded his head. "You did all you could," she said softly. "Let's go home." She escorted him back to the car, and they drove away.

Gloria sat at the kitchen table, reading the Bible. She leaped to her feet when she heard Will's footsteps on the porch. She yelled anxiously before Will could break the plane of the door, "Did you find him?"

Will walked in the door soaking wet, trying not to show his sadness by looking to the ground. He said somberly, "No."

"Oh you poor baby," she said. He sat down at the table, and she brought him a blanket to wrap around him. "Don't you worry about your father. He's going to do everything in his power to try and bring everyone in his group back home safe. We should trust in the Lord and know that he is going to take care of your father, but most importantly we should pray for his safe return home every day," Gloria implored."I know, Mom. I know," Will said, agreeing.

"Things aren't going to be the same without your father here," Gloria said with tears in her eyes.

Will smiled. "Yeah, it's going to be a lot quieter," he said, trying to make light of the situation. "'Will, what is that you have on,'" he mocked his father, "'walking around here like some hippie. Be a man, boy. Get yourself together. When are you going to get a real job and stop playing music all day?'"

Gloria smiled and nudged him on the head. "Boy, go get out of those wet clothes, in here dripping all over my floor." She shook her head and smiled as he trudged down the hall and into his bedroom.

Chapter Nine

Wanton stared into empty space as he remembered the events in his life that had led to his joining the army. Wanton, a brilliant young man, had completed high school in the top of his class and was attending college when he met Gloria. It was like love at first sight. Wanton remembered walking into a café, seeing the most beautiful girl in the world and falling head over heels in love with her. He smiled as he thought about their first kiss and the birth of their son, Will.

Wanton had received his associate's degree before learning that Gloria was pregnant. Wanton wanted to be a great man like he heard his father was, although he had never met him. He married Gloria in hopes of being a great husband and father, so he quit school to provide for his family.

He'd gotten a job as a railroad laborer for the Burlington rail line. He found the wages were not compatible with the labor, so he confronted the supervisor and asked for either better compensation or a management job. Wanton was fired from the job for being too ambitious or perhaps too smart to know that he was more valuable than the money they paid him. In an act of desperation, Wanton joined the army and found the job perfect for him.

In the army, Wanton developed an undying love for his country and found a place where he was awarded and appreciated for his hard work. Wanton quickly rose through the ranks and dedicated his life to the service of his country.

Will gazed into space as his band rehearsed at Club 6661. Pee Wee nudged him, trying to snap him out of the trance he seemed to be in, but it didn't work.

"Hold on, hold on." Pee Wee signaled the band to stop playing. "Just a minute, guys." The band left the stage to get a breather.

Once Pee Wee and Will were alone on stage, Pee Wee confronted Will. "Come on, man, we have to finish this album in a couple of weeks. We need to get it together, and you need to get with the program."

"Pee Wee, I'm just not feeling it, man," Will replied.

"Well, what's wrong?" Pee Wee asked.

"I don't know. I just . . . I just feel like I lost my soul. My heart isn't into the music anymore." He didn't want anyone to know, but his heart was in Korea with his father. Will's nightmares were back and more vivid than ever. He was losing sleep and was being drawn into a deep depression, rapidly losing interest in everything. He was afraid to talk to anyone about it because he didn't believe anyone would understand.

Many people lost their loved ones to the confrontation in Korea, but none was more affected than Will. Although Will and his father never agreed on much, they loved one another more than their personalities could ever show.

"Well, I don't know about you, but I am here for the people," Pee Wee declared. "Through our music, we can send a message of hope! We can give the world what it needs by bringing people together with songs for the soul."

The conversation with Pee Wee reminded Will of the great Dr. Davis, when he once told him a passage according to the Word: "In the same way the spirit helps us in our weakness, we do not know what we ought to pray for, but the spirit himself intercedes for God's people in accordance with the word of God."

"Pray for better days, salvation of the soul, and let the Holy Spirit guide us through our God-given talents," Will murmured.

"Are you good now?" Pee Wee asked. Will nodded his head and Pee Wee threw his hands in the air. "Then let's get this party started." He called the band back to the stage.

Standing tall in the middle of a rice paddy, SFC Wanton watched as his exhausted soldiers filed into formation to hear the rest of his directives for the mission.

"Gentlemen, today is the day we must put our differences aside and work together in order to leave this place in the same manner as which we came. I know many of you are wondering, why are we here? The answer to that burning question is . . . it doesn't matter why we are here. The only thing that matters now is that we are here and doing what it takes to get back in the same condition we came," commanded Wanton. "Teamwork is key to our safe return. I know you guys are tired, but we still have lots of work to do before we can get rest. For those who are not going out on patrol, continue to work on your fighting positions, and I will take the first two squads out on patrol to get an idea of what we are in for. We will move out in the darkest part of the night, so those who are going out with me, get some rest."

The men that weren't going on patrol began to work on their fighting positions.

Pvt. Kennedy turned to Jamal. "Man, I can't believe they have us here fighting in this foreign land."

"I know," Jamal said. "We don't have a dog in this fight. So, why are we here?"

Batts overheard the conversation and interrupted him. "We are here because our country asked us to be here; that is all we need to know."

The soldiers in the bunker winded down after a long day of travel and unpacking. Professor and a few white soldiers read books while lying on their cots. Preach read his Bible as usual, while Pvts. Jamal, Platt, Kennedy, and Cpl. Batts sat around a table made of ammo cans playing cards. The room was fairly quiet with a sense of tension in the air as the realization of their new circumstances set in.

"Can you guys believe this shit, we are here in Korea?" Kennedy said.

"Naw, this is probably some kind of exercise," Platt replied as he tossed a card into the middle of the table. "I mean, don't they have to tell us for sure if this is the real thing?"

Jamal grimaced. "I haven't been to war, but this place feels kind of eerie to me. What do you think, Corporal?"

"I think we should stop worrying about where we are and focus on doing what we need to do to get out of here," Batts replied. "What Wanton said is right. The only thing that matters is getting out of here in the same way we came. It's better not to make assumptions. The only one I'd make right now is to always assume getting home depends upon how you handle yourself out there."

Jamal slammed a card down on the table. "Ace of spades! You can't trump that!"

Platt jumped on top of a trunk. "Snake! Snake!" he yelled.

Jamal leaped onto the table then jumped across the ground to a nearby trunk. Kennedy and Corporal Batts also jumped onto adjacent trunks. The guys in their beds laughed at them.

"What y'all laughing at? Somebody kill that motherfucker! Kill that motherfucker!" Jamal screamed.

Smith calmly got out of his bed, walked over to the snake, and picked him up near the head. "Aw, he is harmless," he said, holding the snake in the air. "He wouldn't hurt a soul." He made a kissing sound with his lips. "You're just a baby, aren't you?"

Jamal, frightened by the snake, screamed, "Get that motherfucker out of here! Get him out!"

"Now, Pvt. Smith!" Batts ordered.

Smith took the snake outside and came back without it a few minutes later. He got back onto his bunk and stretched out.

"Is he gone?" Platt asked. "That thing was at least four feet long. Talking about a baby . . ."

"Yeah, I got rid of him," Smith replied. He rubbed his hands together as if wiping them clean.

There was a general sigh of relief. The men resumed their positions in the bunker, putting their feet back on the ground and going back to what they were doing before.

"Damn, that was a big-ass snake," Johnson said.

"You white motherfuckers. You all are crazy as hell," Jamal said.

Johnson agreed. "Ain't no way in hell I would have touched that big-ass snake. Looked like its head was big as my fist."

"Aw, it was just a snake. It will not bite unless you mess with it. Snakes are more afraid of you than you are of them," Smith said as he pretended to yawn.

"So Smith, what did you do with it?" Platt asked.

"I threw it out."

"What?" Platt asked, "You mean you didn't kill it and there is a snake roaming around here somewhere?"

Smith nodded. "Yes."

"Ain't that a bitch," Jamal said. "I tell you what, if that damn snake bites me, I am going to bite your ass."

Lt. Dukes and SFC Wanton sat in their bunker looking at a map, discussing possible routes to take on their recon mission.

"Sir, I suggest we take this route," suggested Wanton, pointing at the map, "through the jungle to the village.""Sergeant! You need to get your head out of your ass," Dukes insisted. "Why in the hell would I lead these men through a jungle when there is a perfectly good road we can take?""Sir, we just got here and we don't know what is out there yet. We need to proceed with caution," explained Wanton.

"Sergeant, use a little common sense. Oh, I forgot. Common sense isn't common," he hissed as he spat on the ground. "Especially among *your* people. Sergeant, how do you think we are going to get supplies?"

"Sir, they will be flown in just like we were," said Wanton.

"Let me make this simple and easy for you, Sergeant. We are going to do things my way . . . you know why . . . I'll tell you why. I am an officer and you are an NCO, and I was born to lead," explained Dukes.

"Sir, you are going to lead us to certain death if you march us down that road," implored Wanton.

"Wanton, you're making this more difficult than it needs to be, so instead of getting on my nerves in here, go and ready the troops for this mission," commanded Dukes. Wanton stormed out of the bunker while Dukes continued to plot a course for their mission. Wanton and the soldiers stood outside the bunker waiting on Dukes.

Dukes finally emerged from the bunker in full combat gear, yelling, "Move them out, Sergeant."

Wanton marched the soldiers down the road until they left the camp, then he led the troops through the jungle.

"Sergeant Wanton! Hold up," commanded Dukes.

Wanton held his fist up in the air, signaling the men to stop. Dukes came over to him. "What in the hell are you doing? Didn't I tell you we are going via the road? It will lead us straight to the village."

"But sir," appealed Wanton.

"Do as I tell you, Sergeant," Dukes commanded. The white soldiers chuckled a little to see the power Dukes had over Wanton.

SFC Wanton separated the soldiers into two groups, one file on each side of the road.

"All right, guys, settle down and spread out. Keep your guards up," Wanton instructed.

"Can you believe it? We are here in another country," Kennedy said.

"It kind of reminds me of home," Johnson said.

"Yeah," Smith said. "My dad and I used to go hunting in places like this all the time."

"I hate to burst your bubble," Batts said, "but this is combat, not a hunting trip."

"This shit is crazy," Kennedy muttered.

"You got that right," Platt said.

"We are here in a foreign country fighting for the freedom of another country, and we are not free in our own country," Jamal said. "And I don't care what they say about this integration stuff, that's probably not going to last long. Just something they did for appearances sake."

"Keep it down," Wanton hissed.

"These people have not done anything to us," Platt said.

Preach spoke up. "Well, I am a man of the Lord, and it is against my religion to kill."

A bullet hit a soldier walking on Preach's left. Preach yelled, "Oh, goddamn!" as bullets and artillery rounds came from everywhere. Lt. Dukes panicked. SFC Wanton tackled the lieutenant, shoving him to the ground to keep him from being hit by a bullet.

"Get down!" Wanton screamed.

All the soldiers dropped to the ground.

Preach panicked. "These motherfuckers are crazy!"

Wanton gave orders. "Pvt. Johnson, lay down some suppressive fire with that 60. Let's take these motherfuckers out!" SFC Wanton threw a smoke grenade to conceal his men, and they attacked.

The soldiers forgot about their racial differences as they worked together to combat the Korean soldiers, who flanked them on both sides of the road. For the first time, the troops worked with precision;

color was the least of their worries. Survival outweighed all differences they may have had in the United States. They yelled out to one another to indicate their movement: *buddy, move, I got you covered*.

Pvt. Johnson killed four enemy soldiers and threw a grenade into the enemy's fighting position to take out the soldier's rocket launcher.

Wanton shouted, "Everyone, hold your positions. Squad leaders, I need an accountability check of personnel and equipment."

Corporal Batts went to the two squad leaders and received the report, then ran back up to SFC Wanton.

"Sarge, we have one dead and two wounded pretty bad," reported Batts.

An angry Wanton stormed over to Dukes and snatched him by the collar. The black soldiers were shocked and proud to see their black NCO snatch a white officer by the collar with no fear of repercussions.

The white soldiers were equally surprised to see a black man put hands on a white man, to say the least a superior officer, but they understood they were in a foreign country and the rules were a little different.

All the soldiers understood Wanton was full of passion and cared for them deeply, and he didn't care about any race or rank. The only thing that mattered to him in the current situation was the well-being of his soldiers. The skirmish made it clear, they needed one another to survive their current situation.

SFC Wanton screamed, "Because of you, some of my men are not going to see their families again! This is not a game!"

Dukes gives little resistance to Wanton, partly out of fear. No man of color had ever touched him in such a way in the United States; he was protected by the Jim Crow laws that would give him the right to retaliate. On the battlefield, there were no such laws; the only thing that mattered was survival, and that eliminated racism. Filled with guilt, Dukes listen with complete attention as Wanton laid down his laws on the battlefield.

"If you cause any more of my men to get hurt again, you will be the one going back in a body bag, and I'll be the one to put you in it," Wanton hissed. "Is that understood, sir?" Wanton pushed Dukes onto the ground.

The embarrassed Dukes got up, dusted himself off, and stated calmly, "Let's continue the mission."Wanton moved back to point position and signaled the men to form a wedge formation. Wanton led the men from the road and through the jungle toward the hill until SFC Wanton raised his fist, signaling them to stop once he reached the top of the hill. He pulled his binoculars, took a look, and then signaled for Dukes.

"Take a look, sir," Wanton told him. Dukes looked through the binoculars.

"Holy shit," Dukes said.

The city at the bottom of the hills was in ruins. Some buildings were burned out, others still on fire---yet other houses looked as if they had been taken out by bombs. Only one house remained standing with a single light on inside.

"Looks like they were hit pretty bad. Do you see any signs of enemy activity?" asked Wanton.

"Negative."

"Sir, it's your move," Wanton requested.

Dukes turned and motioned for Batts to join them. He ran to their side.

"Corporal, watch for enemy activity in the town below while SFC Wanton and I brief the soldiers on their recon mission."

"Yes, Lieutenant!"

Dukes and Wanton moved a fourth of the way back down the hill and then signaled for their men to rally around them. They debriefed with the soldiers, telling them their plans to go down to the desolate city below, collect intel, and return to base. The soldiers carefully descended the hill and stopped at its base.

Pointing at the destruction of some of the buildings, Wanton said, "Looks like we had a brigade of light infantrymen headed east through this town, and judging by the looks of things, their heavy armor and artillery are not far away.""Well, let's do a quick recon and get the hell out of here," implored Dukes.

"Sounds good to me, sir," replied Wanton. He signaled the soldiers to form a column of twos. The soldiers spread out to do recon. In the city, the air was thick with smoke, and the smell of death filled the air. Mangled bodies and debris were strewn everywhere. Some of the men had to fight the urge to gag. Johnson made a choking sound in the back of his throat. "Man, don't you start that shit," Jamal threatened between gritted teeth. "You puke out here like a little girl, I swear I'll shoot you myself."

When they reached the middle of the city, Wanton signaled for the men to stop again. "We need a bird's-eye view," Wanton said, turning to Dukes. "What do you suggest, sir?"

"Barely anything left in this town," Dukes said. "I guess we can try that one over there."

He pointed toward a building that was so decimated it was hard to tell what it once had been. Wanton and Dukes went in, stepping through the piles of smoldering waste and ashes inside. There was no railing, but the stairway was mostly intact, except for a broken step near the bottom. Wanton made it up to the second-floor window first.

"You'd better see this," he said.

"You can't just tell me what you see . . . ?" Dukes asked. His voice trailed off as he stood next to Wanton and looked down.

The window was so narrow that they had to stand with their bodies pressed shoulder to shoulder in order to both look at the same time. They could see a tank battalion and some light infantrymen headed toward them.

"Holy shit!" Dukes cried.

"We've got to get the hell out of here," Wanton said.

They ran down the stairs, and once outside, both Wanton and Dukes maintained their stony expressions. Wanton gave the orders—the men were to follow as they made a quick exit of the city. The soldiers kept their heads down and followed orders. No one had to tell them that something had just changed.

They strategically moved through the city. Wanton kept looking around, and his men did as well.

"We're close," Dukes said. "Something doesn't feel right."

Just as they were about to clear one last corner, the men paused. They heard the sounds of heavy machinery before they actually saw them rumbling through the city. Wanton gave the command to fall back, but there was nowhere for them to go.

A tank stopped, and a machine gun on top broke the silence with a flurry of shots toward them.

The men returned fire and then ran for cover as best as they could; some flew through the doorways of abandoned buildings; others went through windows. North Korean infantry soldiers gathered, their commander giving one order: search the abandoned buildings to capture the American soldiers or take them out.

After breaking in through a window, Jamal, Platt, Smith, Hamilton, and a handful of other soldiers moved slowly through a building.

"I wish I knew where the hell we were going," Hamilton said.

"You wouldn't be the only one," Smith said. "Anywhere away from those sons of a bitches sounds good about now."

"No kidding," Platt said sarcastically. "I want to know where they came from. It's like they just appeared . . ."

Jamal stopped in his tracks. "Hear that?"

"Hear what?" Hamilton asked.

Just as Smith was about to say no, he heard footsteps. He turned toward the back door, and his glance was met with the barrel of a gun. Jamal leaped in an effort to shield Smith and Hamilton from the bullet aimed at them. While Jamal rolled on the floor screaming in pain and clutching his chest, Smith rolled and pointed his weapon at the Korean soldier in the door and shot him. Hamilton and Smith fought with the enemy soldiers as Platt tried to treat Jamal's wound and silence him.

Once they had their skirmish under control, Smith and Hamilton rushed over to see how Jamal was doing.

Jamal opened his eyes, grimacing in pain. "What in the fuck are y'all looking at? You act like you have never seen a man shot before. Help me up and let's get the fuck out of here!"

Smith and Hamilton smiled when they heard the profane words from Jamal's mouth.

Johnson, the machine gunner, lay on the ground in the prone position, providing cover for his fellow soldiers as they retreated from the hostile fire. The North Koreans were in pursuit and angry because several of their comrades had been mowed down.

One American soldier fell to the ground as he was hit in the back by a stray bullet. Another was hit in the leg, but he grabbed it and continued to hop to their rally point to wait on the rest of the soldiers.

The enemy soldiers advanced slowly. Some of the soldiers ran into the only building in the entire city that had lights, but several buildings were still intact. They maneuvered their way out of the buildings and back to the bottom of the hill.

Lt. Dukes called the men to order. "Where is SFC Wanton?" he demanded.

Corporal Batts shook his head. "We don't know."

"Fuck!" Dukes cried, mopping his forehead with the back of his hand. "Okay, here's what's going to happen. Batts, if I don't come back here with SFC Wanton in exactly five minutes, call in for air support to bomb the city. Give me that map," he said, snatching the paper from one soldier's hands. He pulled a pencil from his pocket and scribbled.

"Here are the coordinates. Tell them we are under heavy fire from a tank battalion and some light infantrymen attacking from the west." When he was done with the map, he shoved it at Batts. "Got it?" Dukes asked.

"Yes, sir!" Batts said. Lt. Dukes turned to walk away.

"Sir!" Batts called behind him.

"Yes?" Dukes turned.

"Good luck."

Lt. Dukes ran back toward the city, attempting to move undetected, slipping between shadows and doorways, his every sense alert to the sounds of enemy soldiers or the rumbling of tanks. There was noise everywhere, and at times Dukes was not sure where the noises were coming from. One wrong turn and he could walk straight into a nest of enemy soldiers. He promised himself they wouldn't take him alive if it came to that.

He took in a deep breath. It hadn't come to that yet. He still had a job to do.

Checking his watch, he saw that he'd somehow managed to break the face of it. The tiny hands were smashed. There was no way to know how many minutes he'd been searching for Wanton, but it felt like way too long. Cutting through streets, peeking through alleys, he was about to turn back when he saw a movement from the corner of his eye.

An American soldier staggered down the middle of the street, his face caked in dirt and blood. He carried his gun over his shoulder and bit down on his lip as he dragged his left leg.

A rumble filled the earth beneath them. Dukes watched in horror as a tank turned the corner and pulled out into the middle of the intersection behind the injured soldier.

"Wanton!" Dukes cried. He ran toward his comrade.

And then another sound, from above. A helicopter. He looked up and saw the air cav roaring through the sky like an angry beast. The whistling hiss that followed reminded Dukes of fireworks. A rocket sailed down from the helicopter and hit the tank. The explosion shook the ground and knocked both men off their feet. Once Dukes climbed to his feet, he ran toward Wanton.

"I got you, Sarge," he said, pulling Wanton up. "I got you."

The two men ran together toward the bottom of the hill and met with the rest of the troops.

"Still behind us?" Wanton asked, panting for breath.

Dukes laughed. "I think the air cav is gonna keep them busy for a while."

Several other soldiers came to meet them halfway down the hill. The men hooted with joy to see both Wanton and Dukes had survived. "Report. Somebody better tell me something," Dukes barked as the troops hurried to account for everyone and prepare the injured to be airlifted out.

SFC Wanton lay in bed with heavy bandages over his eyes. He had been in and out of consciousness for the last day. He was disoriented and didn't know where he was or why he was there. At first, he thought he might be in Korea, a hostage with something over his eyes. But his calls for help had quickly alerted the nurse. Speaking in a warm southern accent, she told him that he was indeed in a hospital room at Camp Campbell. The bandages were only to protect his eyes while they healed. The explosion had caused temporary blindness, along with a myriad of cuts, scrapes, and a burn on his left hand.

The doctor was called to his bedside immediately. Wanton had injured his right leg, and though there was some damage, the doctor explained he would have mobility but might have a slight limp once it healed. "It will be almost unnoticeable," the doctor said. "You'll still be able to dance with your wife."

"Gloria would be shocked," Wanton said. "We haven't danced together since our wedding."

"You've still got a sense of humor," the doctor said. "That's a very good sign, Sergeant. You need your rest, and then tomorrow we'll see how you're feeling. I don't expect that you will have to stay with us for long."

The nurse administered another sedative to help him sleep. Though he rested peacefully most of the night, he fell into a strange bout of dreams toward dawn—vague visions of a burning city and the sound of gunfire, the smell of death and the rumble of tanks moving over the ground. He remembered the sound of a tank drawing close and the terrified expression on Dukes's face as he ran toward him, screaming at the top of his lungs.

The next evening, Lt. Dukes walked into the room and stood at the bedside. "How's my top NCO?"

Wanton smiled. "A lot better when I get out of this bed. So how is the war going?"

"It's over," Dukes said. "We did very well."

"How are the guys?" Wanton asked. Dukes caught a note of apprehension in his voice. As hard as he could be on them, he loved those boys like they were his own sons.

"They are fine. Everyone made it out okay. We only had some minor injuries, thanks to you," Dukes said. He pulled up a chair from the corner of the room and sat down. "Sergeant Wanton, I came here to thank you. I want to thank you for sharing your tactical skills, but most importantly, I want to thank you for teaching me about life."

"Awww . . . sir . . . come on," Wanton started.

"Just hear me out, Sergeant. Because of you, I understand Lincoln's saying 'A house divided against itself cannot stand.' You and I, we are just a small part of this country, and when we worked together we accomplished great things. Just think of how great this country could be if all races, religions, and genders of this country could work together. It is sad to say, but it took adversity to pull us together. It is when we stand united that we are the greatest America."

The same evening, across town, Pvt. Smith and Pvt. Jamal walked down the street together wearing their uniforms.

"My family owns a manufacturing business on the north side of town, and we also own this restaurant," Smith explained. "Let's get something to eat, my treat."

Jamal paused. In the window next to the front door sat a huge sign: NO COLOREDS ALLOWED.

"Uh, man, I can't go in there." Jamal shifted uncomfortably.

"Yes you can," Smith said, opening the door. "Come on in; you are going to love the food."

The two found a booth and Jamal sat down. "I'll be back," Smith said. "Men's room."

Smith walked past the counter, and a pudgy, middle-aged blonde lady came running at him. She wiped her hands on an apron.

"John, is that you?" she said.

"Yes, ma'am, Aunt Bessie."

"Well, I do declare, when did you get back? This is such a nice surprise!"

"A couple of days ago." Smith grinned.

"You sure look good in that there uniform. Just like your grandfather. He'd be so proud." She beamed.

"Thank you, Aunt Bessie." Smith continued to the restroom.

Tapping his fingers against the table, Jamal picked up a dessert menu from the side of the table and leafed through the pages. Someone cleared their throat and he looked up. He was flanked by two rednecks. One of them put his foot up on the seat across from Jamal.

"Hey boy, you shell shocked or something? Or just *stupid*?"

Jamal looked up at the men. Clenching his fist, he pretended to look down at the menu again.

"You hear me, boy? Your kind are not allowed in here," the man continued.

"Says who?" asked Smith.

The men turned around and saw Smith standing behind them.

"Welcome back, John. We were just telling this here boy that he cannot eat here," explained Bobby.

"I invited him here, and he can come here anytime he wishes," said Smith.

"What are you talking about?" asked Bobby. "Coloreds can't eat here. It's the law; it even says so in the window."

"Well, that law doesn't apply here, and especially not to this man. You see that uniform? While you and the rest of these pansy asses were here eating steak and sleeping in a warm bed every night, this man right here put his life on the line for this country for the sake of the freedoms that your sorry ass enjoys. Instead of harassing him, you should be thanking him . . . and if you don't like the thought of a colored person eating at this here restaurant, you can get the hell out because this man stays. And from this day forward, this restaurant will not refuse service to anyone because of the color of their skin."

The two white men walked out, followed by a few others.

Smith walked over to the window. "Hey," he called, "take this with you," he said, and tossed the "NO BLACKS ALLOWED" sign out onto the street. He casually walked back to the table, straightened his tie, and sat down across from his friend.

Jamal was silent for a moment, stunned at the courage Smith displayed on his behalf.

"You know they are going to try and ruin your business because of you calling me your friend," Jamal explained.Smith smiled. "They are the least of my worries. We have more important work to do."

Jamal puzzled, "We! What do you mean we?"

"Yes, I am talking about us. We still have some fighting to do," explained Smith.

"I am not going to serve another term, no sir," Jamal expressed.

"No, man. I am not talking about the military, I am talking about fighting Jim Crow," Smith explained.

"Now that is the kind of war I am ready to fight," Jamal replied.

"Aunt Bessie," Smith called, "can we have a couple glasses of water? And two dinner menus?"

"So, where's our son?" SFC Wanton asked. Gloria had come to visit him in the hospital, and she sat beside his bed.

"Oh, he is out of town doing a concert. You will be so proud of him," she said warmly.

"Does he know that I am here?"

"No, he's going to be so excited to see you once he knows you're back home."

"When's he going to be back?" Wanton asked.

Gloria didn't have a chance to answer. Just then, a group of handsome young men in uniform walked in. It was the entire platoon. The guys came in and crowded around the bed in a semicircle.

"Get up, you maggot," Jamal teased the sergeant.

"This ain't a motel," Platt added.

"Real soldiers don't *get* tired," Kennedy said.

Jamal took Gloria's hand. "And who is this lovely lady?"

"Don't make me get out this bed," Wanton threatened.

"Slow your roll, Sarge. We just came to get you out of bed," Jamal replied, but not before he kissed Gloria's hand.

Pvt. Platt opened Wanton's locker and pulled out his Class A uniform. The guys helped Wanton put it on. Mrs. Wanton looked on and smiled. "You look so handsome."

"Are you ready for this?" Batts asked.

"For what?" Wanton said.

Doc began to unwrap the bandage from around his eyes.

"Are you guys authorized to do this?"

"No, but we take care of our own," Doc replied.

Once the bandages were off, SFC Wanton closed his eyes and covered them with his hands. "Oh, it's too bright. The doctors said they will be sore for a while."

Gloria rubbed his shoulders. "I just thank God you're okay and the blindness is only temporary," she said.

"Things will be blurry for a while, so keep these sunglasses on," said the doctor, putting the shades on Wanton's eyes.

"Come on, Sarge, let's go," Jamal said. "We have places to go and things to do."

Club 1999 was packed with people. The soldiers walked in, taking seats near the back of the club. Wanton sat between Jamal and Gloria. Though he could not see his son, he smiled when he heard his voice. Bertha and Karen were in the club as well, sitting at a table closer to the stage.

Will, Pee Wee, and their band were onstage. As the music played, a spotlight shined on Will.

Will looked out into the audience, his eyes wide and faraway. With the bright light on him, he only saw the shapes of people in the audience. Not being able to see clearly out into the audience added to the surreal feeling of performing for a packed club. "You know in John 3:16 it states, 'For God so loved the world that he gave his only begotten son, so that whosoever believes in him shall not perish but should have everlasting life.' So, I ask you tonight, are you willing to make sacrifices for those things that you love or those things that you believe in? You know, I used to have nightmares about my father dying in war, and my mom used to hold me and say . . ."

Will took a breath, and his warm tenor poured through the room, singing the lyrics of his new song:

Try to sleep relax your mind. Don't worry about the fighting it will all end in time.

Cry not for your sadness, laugh at the pain.

Pray for better days may freedom reign.

As Will sang the song, Gloria slowly led Wanton to the stage. Tears ran down both their eyes as Will and his dad recognized one another.

www.ingramcontent.com/pod-product-compliance
Lightning Source LLC
Chambersburg PA
CBHW060122260626
47160CB00005B/1977